The Wary Heart

by
Lynn Granger

Dales Large Print Books
Long Preston, North Yorkshire,
England.

British Library Cataloguing in Publication Data.

Granger, Lynn
The wary heart.

A catalogue record for this book is
available from the British Library

ISBN 1-85389-642-X pbk

First published in Great Britain by Robert Hale Ltd., 1987

Copyright © 1987 by Lynn Granger

The right of Lynn Granger to be identified as the author of
this work has been asserted in accordance with the Copyright,
Designs and Patents Act, 1988

Published in Large Print July, 1996 by arrangement with
Robert Hale Ltd.

Dales Large Print is an imprint of
Library Magna Books Ltd.
Printed and bound in Great Britain by
T.J. Press (Padstow) Ltd., Cornwall, PL28 8RW.

THE WARY HEART

Jan Carron owes her sister a favour, so when Chris asks her to look after her children at Shamlee, their Scottish farm, Jan promises to go. Jonathan White is so disgruntled at her decision that Jan wonders if he really loves her. Dark and moody Mike Maxwell is also at Shamlee. Mike disapproves of Jonathan and of Jan's friendship with the local vet, Timothy Greig. Yet Mike makes no secret of his attachment to his friend's wife Angela McCall whose son bears an uncanny resemblance both to Mike and to four year old Bobby Carron.

The Penalty of Love

If love should count you worthy, and
  should deign
One day to seek your door and be your
  guest,
Pause! ere you draw the bolt and bid
  him rest,
If in your old content you would remain,
For not alone he enters; in his train
Are angels of the mist, the lonely guest
Dreams of the unfulfilled and unpossessed,
And sorrow, and Life's immemorial pain.

He wakes desires you never may forget,
He shows you stars you never saw before,
He makes you share with him, for
  evermore,
The burden of the world's divine regret.
How wise you were to open not! and yet,
How poor if you should turn him from
  the door!

Sidney Royse Lysaght.

Chapter One

Sorting through the treasures and trivia accumulated by three generations of Carrons was proving just as agonising as Jan had feared. Perhaps John had been right after all. Maybe it had been a mistake to keep back the farm cottage from the sale. Certainly it was far too small to hold half the things she longed to keep—not to mention Bobby's pedal tractor and the rest of his cherished toys. But even worse was the prospect of the new owners taking over her beloved Cherrytrees and watching the inevitable changes.

Along with her sister, Christine, Jan had spent an idyllic childhood on the small Yorkshire farm where her father and grandfather had been born. She knew and loved every field and stream, every hedge and tree.

The shrill ring of the telephone brought her sharply from her knees beside the bulging packing cases. She hated the sound of its sinister summons since the dreadful night she had answered it six months ago. The night on which she had learned that her parents had been killed in a tragically simple accident. Her feet clattered eerily on the bare floor boards where she had already removed the carpets. The sound made the old house seem empty and forlorn and its desolation found an echo in her own heart.

At the bottom of the stairs she glanced at the brass face of the grandfather clock still standing in the hall, steadily ticking away the minutes. It was well after ten o'clock. She grabbed the telephone receiver, silencing its strident shrill.

'Chris!' Her tone registered surprise. 'Is...is anything wrong?' Ever since her sister had married Tom Kerr and gone to live in Scotland she had phoned home to Cherrytrees every Sunday afternoon. It was a ritual she had faithfully continued since the death of their parents. But today was only Tuesday...

'No, there's nothing wrong, Jan. I didn't mean to alarm you. I have some good news for once—or at least Tom has.'

'Whew, that's a relief!' Jan flopped weakly onto the old oak settle. 'Right...I'm all ears!'

8

Chris's warm chuckle came clearly over the wire. 'I had to wait until the twins were in bed. I'm sure Julie and Billy have more energy than a whole class of four-year-olds! Then Tom and I and Papa Kerr had a long discussion—that's why I'm so late phoning...'

'Come on, Chris! Spill the beans,' Jan laughed in a fever of impatience.

'Right—Tom has been invited to go on a lecture-cum-study tour in the United States!'

'Oh Chris! That's wonderful. He never dreamed he would get a second chance, did he? But...er what does Papa Kerr think about it?' William Kerr was Tom's father but he had been Papa Kerr to them all since his twin grandchildren began to talk. He was presently recovering from the second of two very serious heart-attacks.

'Well, that's the amazing thing, Jan,' Chris continued excitedly, 'He is *insisting* that Tom should grasp the opportunity this time... We knew his views had changed radically during his long stay in hospital of course. He seems to have realised that Tom's talents lay in genetic research rather than in farming Shamlee.'

'I'm so glad,' Jan said warmly.

She knew Tom had received a similar offer five years ago—only a few months after he and Chris were married. After a great deal of soul-searching he had reluctantly turned it down, knowing he couldn't upset his father by leaving Shamlee so soon after Mike, his foster-brother.

Mike Maxwell had been the one who had truly shared William Kerr's lifelong interest in Shamlee and in the breeding of pedigree cattle. Jan pictured him clearly—his green eyes gleaming and gold-flecked with laughter, full of intimate secrets. Secrets he might share with warmth and love if ever he found the woman he could trust with his wary heart. She shivered involuntarily. The last time she had seen him his eyes were bleak and grey—disillusioned? frustrated? angry?—all of those—but surely there had been something more, something deeper, almost vulnerable beneath his proud and arrogant manner? But five years ago she had been too young and inexperienced to cope with the unexpected tide of her own emotions—much less those of a man as complex as Mike Maxwell. His sudden decision to go off to Canada had surprised everyone.

Tom had done his best to settle down to the running of Shamlee while managing to keep abreast of the rapidly developing world of embryo transplants and genetic research. Jan liked her blond, good-natured brother-in-law and her congratulations were sincere.

'Unfortunately there is a snag—' Chris admitted slowly, 'Tom wants me to accompany him. I must confess I dread the prospect of parting—but I can't possibly take the twins, especially at the beginning while he is travelling most of the time...' She sighed heavily, 'If only we had Mum...'

'I know, Chris, I know...' She heard the tremor in her own voice. 'There's Papa Kerr too,' Chris went on slowly, then in a sudden rush, 'he asked me to make a proposition to you, Jan. But honestly I don't blame you for refusing. I know how hard it would be to get another job afterwards...'

'Chris! What sort of proposition? What are you trying to tell me?' Jan prompted patiently, knowing her sister's propensity for rambling round a subject if she was worried or excited. Right now she was both, and, not for the first time, Jan felt more like the elder 'sister in charge'.

'We-ell, Papa Kerr thinks you are the only person we could trust with the twins—and of course himself. He has always enjoyed your company, as you must know. He wondered if you would consider coming here—to Shamlee, if I go with Tom. He, indeed we all, think it might be good for you to get away from Cherrytrees for a while. But I know how hard you have worked at the laboratory. It wouldn't be easy to get another job where the boss allowed you a free hand as Vic Thomson does...'

It certainly would not! Jan agreed silently, virtually impossible in fact. But she owed Chris so much...a debt she could never fully repay—and there was no one else to help out now. Chris was still missing their parents as much as herself and Bobby. She could not stand aloof.

'Jan?' Chris murmured tentatively, 'Please don't worry. We understand...'

Jan's teeth bit hard on her full lower lip. She took a deep breath.

'I'll tell Vic Thomson first thing in the morning,' she promised. 'Everything will work out fine. You go ahead and make your plans to go with Tom—he's much too handsome to be allowed away on his own.' She tried hard to instill some humour into the conversation to cover her own doubts.

Vic Thomson was the over-all manager in the creamery where she had charge of the milk-testing laboratory. He had been exceptionally good to her during the past six months.

'And what about John?' Chris persisted anxiously. 'How will he feel about you spending six months in Scotland?'

Jan frowned and chewed harder than ever on her poor lips but she finally suceeded in convincing Chris that everything would be all right.

Johnathan White was the assistant manager at the creamery. They had dated spasmodically over the past three years but since the death of her parents he had been extra attentive. He had taken a lot of trouble to get the best auctioneers for the sale of Cherrytrees. He had never liked the cattle but he had helped tirelessly with the phenomenal amount of work involved in cataloguing the pedigrees and researching the background breeding which had made the sale of her father's herd realise its true value.

Yes, John would not be pleased at her decision. Several times recently he had tried to persuade her to fix a date for their wedding. His love-making was becoming increasingly ardent and impatient. Only a few days ago he had accused her of being frigid. But she had not always been frigid... Her relationship with Johnathan lacked that vital spark which had once transported her, however briefly, into another world.

Unbidden, definitely unwelcome, a picture of Chris's wedding day sprang to mind. Vividly she recalled the tall kilted figure of Tom's best man, Mike Maxwell. She remembered the lean determined jaw, the crooked smile which revealed his strong white teeth against a skin permanently tanned by his love of the outdoor life.

Jan shuddered, remembering the present, precarious state of Papa Kerr's health. A relapse or another heart-attack would bring Mike Maxwell flying back to Shamlee immediately. She knew he had chartered a special flight to reach the old man's bedside the moment he knew his foster parent was in hospital. But he was the last person she wanted to meet. Had she been too hasty in promising Chris she would help? Her conscience allowed no alternative. She could only hope that Papa Kerr's health continued to improve.

Vic Thomson surveyed Jan across the solid width of his desk. He noted the oval face with its high cheekbones, the bell of shining chestnut hair, the strain in her wide grey eyes watching him anxiously through a fringe of curling dark lashes. He sighed. The lass was by far the best he'd had in the laboratory but she'd had more than her fair share of trouble.

'Would you say that assistant of yours— Linda isn't it?—could manage without you for the next few months, lass?' he asked in his blunt, broad Yorkshire accent. Jan looked back at him, a faint hope lightening her expression.

'Yes, I think so, especially now we have the new electronic apparatus for the butterfat testing...and of course we shall have a reduction in the quantity of milk coming in while the new UHT plant is being installed...I'd forgotten that! Yes, I believe Linda would enjoy the challenge now.'

Jan had known Linda Wright for

some years and they had become good friends. Although she had failed her final examinations at college Jan had found her totally competent and reliable in the laboratory. It was typical of Vic Thomson that he should understand this, yet John, whose work as assistant manager, brought him frequently into the laboratory, never seemed to notice Linda at all.

Vic Thomson made a pyramid of his stubby fingers and pondered it thoughtfully.

'Right then, lass,' he said decisively at last, 'I reckon as a change would do yer good. We'll expect yer back for't start up o't UHT plant, eh?' His blue eyes twinkled suddenly, 'That's if them Scotch fellers let yer come back...'

Jan gave him a radiant smile and only just restrained herself from hugging him. She could go to Shamlee and help Chris and she would still have her job when she returned. She could hardly believe that fortune was favouring her at last. She skipped happily down the steps of the office block and all the way across to the laboratories to break the news to Linda.

Vic Thomson watched her slender white-coated figure and the jaunty bounce of her

16

shining hair. He was glad he had been able to put the spring back in her step and see her happy smile again. Everybody, from the women on the bottling plant, to the tanker drivers and office staff had missed her sunny smile. John White was a fool to let her out of his sight and he told him so in his usual forthright style at their regular morning meeting.

As soon as Jan saw Johnathan striding furiously towards the laboratories she realised what had happened. She should have broken the news to Johnathan first, she thought guiltily.

Tactful as always, Linda excused herself, saying she had to take some sterile rinses of a troublesome part of the pasteurising plant. Afterwards Jan was glad Linda had not witnessed John's tirade. Once she had recovered from the initial shock she realised that in the heat of his anger he had shed his charming façade. His true motives and, worse, those of his mother, were painfully revealed.

Amelia White had always regarded the Carron family as little more than peasants. Her own life revolved around the golf club and bridge parties. Two months ago she had moved to a large house, complete with a maid and a gardener—a style ideally suited to her blue-rinsed coiffure and regal bearing, and one she had long craved. She had shown a new friendliness, which Jan had attributed to sympathy, following the death of her parents. Even Bobby was made almost welcome—so long as he behaved like a stuffed doll! Now Jan learned the reason for her changed attitude and John's urgent desire for marriage.

The Whites had both regarded Cherry-trees, with its mortgage, muck and continual hard work, as a despised liability. But they had been quick to assess its potential as saleable property—a comfortable house, the inflated value of land, and because of her parents' death it had vacant possession once she had moved out herself. They had assumed that she would inherit at least half the proceeds. Naturally, as John's wife she would share their new house—and the cost and upkeep of course! Bobby, previously a large thorn in the flesh of both John and his mother, was no longer a problem—he would be packed off to a suitable boarding school!

Jan choked on the bitter irony of it all, remembering John's scrupulous care to extract every last penny out of the cattle he had despised.

John tried to retract his words as soon as he saw Jan's shocked pale face and the disillusion in her expressive eyes. Wearily she pretended to accept his garbled explanations. All she wanted was to be alone. She felt cold and hollow and utterly despondent. The esteem which she had struggled to rebuild so slowly and painfully over the last four years was shattered. John didn't love her—not for herself! Oh, he was attracted by her physical attributes—he had made no secret of his desires—but he had been more attracted once he believed her to be a potential heiress. Now she understood his urgent desire for marriage.

Perhaps Papa Kerr was right. It would be a relief to escape to the peace and tranquillity of Shamlee and the childrens' uncomplicated acceptance. She had intended to ask John to drive her to Scotland but now she made a firm resolve to travel by train. Christine must not be allowed to suspect they had quarrelled.

Jan smiled gratefully at the young man opposite. He had been a cheerful travelling companion and had kept Bobby enthralled

19

with his stories of animals, until the little boy had succumbed to exhaustion and fallen asleep against her arm. She looked down tenderly at the soft rumpled hair and the curve of his flushed cheek.

Timothy Greig took the opportunity for a little gentle scrutiny of his own. He had introduced himself and mentioned his job as a vet, in partnership with his father, just north of the Scottish Border. He had gained little information in return. He studied the delicate profile and the tinge of clear pink colour which emphasised the girl's high cheekbones, the small straight nose and full generous mouth—maybe too wide for true beauty, but very very kissable, Tim concluded with the eye of a connoisseur. He was intrigued by the wide grey eyes with their sooty curling lashes, but that clear direct gaze had somehow deflected his usual brash approach. Nothing could stop him from speculating though. She wore no rings so it seemed reasonable to assume she was not married. Even Tim steered clear of married ladies, however attractive. Her shy reserve and serene smile gave her an untouchable air, yet she obviously cared deeply for the little fellow at her side. But then he was an engaging wee chap,

Tim thought wistfully—bright too, with his wide green eyes sparkling with mischief, and the tiny square teeth revealed by his slightly crooked grin. There was something vaguely familiar, something about the child that tugged at Tim's memory.

'Come on Bobby, wake up now,' Jan murmured coaxingly. 'We are in Scotland already. We must get off at the next station.'

Tim sat up, suddenly alert. 'That's Bayanloch! That's my station!'

Jan gave him a gently teasing smile. 'Well I hope you have no objection to us using it too?' She stood up to stretch her cramped limbs and reach for her holdall.

'No objection at all!' Tim whistled silently, as he gazed appreciatively at her long legs and slim hips in the well-cut green trouser suit. Beneath the open jacket she wore a bright yellow sweater, which gave him only a tantalising glimpse of delectable curves.

Tim lowered his glance as she set the bag on the table between them. 'I will help you off with your luggage,' he offered cheerily, as his eye blatantly scanned the labels.

'Shamlee!' he exclaimed. 'You can't be Chris's sister, surely? Christine Kerr?' He stared at the smooth fall of dark brown hair, gleaming with copper lights in the slanting rays of the September sun. 'Chris is so small and fair!'

Jan smiled slowly. 'We are still sisters though. Do you know the Kerrs well?'

'Know them! I sure do!' He grinned widely. 'So! I shall certainly see you again,' he stated with satisfaction. 'I often call at Shamlee for my morning coffee if I'm working near Westburn village. Tom and Mike are old friends.'

Jan's hand stilled on Bobby's shoulder and some of the warm colour left her face. Even the mention of Mike Maxwell's name set her trembling inwardly. 'I...I am going to look after the twins so that Chris can go with my brother-in-law.' She steadied her voice with an effort. 'You will have heard that Tom is going to America I suppose?'

'Oh yes indeed! He's a clever fellow, our Doctor Tom. Everyone in the Glen is proud of him— Not that Mike is exactly stupid either, but he always did prefer the more practical aspects—the actual breeding of the cattle. I think Mr Kerr always knew in his heart that he would be the one to take over some day. He could buy almost any farm in the area—maybe two or three, I imagine, but he has always loved Shamlee.' Jan felt a shiver of apprehension, as Tim continued cheerfully, 'I don't know why he hopped off to Canada so suddenly, but at least he's here to take over this time and let Tom have his chance.'

Jan's fingers tightened convulsively on Bobby's small shoulder. 'Ouch! You's hurted me!' he protested loudly. Jan turned quickly towards him with the pretext of comfort, successfully hiding her white face and trembling limbs from Timothy Greig's all-seeing eyes. She struggled desperately to control her thumping heart and the surge of breathless panic which threatened to overwhelm her senses. She wanted to turn the train around and go back! Or stay on and keep going and going...Mike back at Shamlee! To stay! It was not possible...

'Are we's nearly there?' Bobby chirped excitedly, now wide awake and full of renewed energy after his nap.

'Aye we are that!' Tim answered him as he concentrated on getting the heavy cases to the door.

Jan pulled Bobby's small anorak on automatically and zipped it up with a jerk, her mind in a turmoil of indecision.

23

The train was slowing. She couldn't leave Chris and Tom in the lurch at this late stage—or could she? There was Bobby to consider too. 'Dear God what can I do?' she prayed silently, in growing desperation as the train lurched, slowed again, then jolted to its brief halt.

Tim Greig lifted Bobby onto the platform and Jan was forced to follow and keep a tight hold on his tiny hand as he wriggled in excitement. The station was small and the train did not linger. Jan looked round wildly. She saw Tom clattering over the wooden bridge. Why, oh why had she assumed Mike had returned to Canada? Why hadn't she considered that Shamlee needed someone to manage the stock and men as well as the house? She had been too absorbed in her own problems to think straight. At all costs she must avoid Mike Maxwell... Her brain whirled as Tom ran down the last few steps, his pleasant face creased in a welcoming grin. He greeted them with his usual warmth before turning to their companion without surprise.

'So you're back from the conference and the bright lights, Tim? Can we offer you a lift?'

'Aye, that would be a grand help. Thanks Tom. I could phone home from Shamlee. It would give me a wee while longer to get to know your charming sister-in-law.' He grinned disarmingly but Jan felt too churned up to offer more than a perfunctory smile.

Together they climbed slowly over the wooden bridge, with Bobby insisting on peering through the cracks at the gleaming lines below.

'Chris will soon stretch the supper for an extra one,' Tom said cheerfully as he heaved the cases into the big boot before settling them in the car, 'And Mike will probably offer to run you home afterwards.'

'Oh better and better. Thanks!' Tim accepted with alacrity, 'Presumably Mike's at home for once then, is he?'

'We-ell,' Tom shrugged uneasily Jan thought as she listened tensely to their conversation. 'He was just coming in from the milking when I left.' Jan felt her chest tighten with panic. Surely she would not have to come into contact with Mike? Her fingers clasped and unclasped the strap of her leather handbag. As though sensing her disquiet, Bobby cuddled close to her on the back seat, temporarily subdued.

Tom concentrated on reversing out of the tiny station yard before resuming his conversation and Jan had the distinct impression that he was weighing his words carefully.

'I'm afraid Mike's continuing association with Mrs McCall is causing father some concern—and worry is the last thing he needs. But Mike has always had a soft spot for Angela, ever since the Dunbars moved to the Glen when she was just a schoolgirl. The trouble is, she shows no indication of returning to her husband—even though her mother has made such an excellent recovery since the removal of the brain tumour.' He sighed heavily.

'Mmm. It's a rare tangle,' Tim agreed. 'After all Jim McCall and Mike were the best of friends. Then there is the boy too...'

Their voices droned on until the car turned into the narrow road leading to Shamlee. Almost before the car had stopped, Chris was pulling open the door, hugging Jan in a warm embrace, before returning her laughing blue eyes to Bobby's small bewildered face. His bottom lip trembled,

26

'I'se want Grampy,' he muttered fretfully. Jan, met her sister's gaze with wide troubled eyes as she stroked Bobby's soft dark hair soothingly.

'It's weeks since he asked for dad,' she murmured with a faint tremor in her own voice.

No mention was made of Mike Maxwell and he was not present at the delicious meal which Chris had prepared. Jan hoped he always ate in his own home, as she began to relax in the friendly atmosphere of Chris's crowded kitchen. The children had settled down to explore each other's toys. Watching the two small fair heads on either side of Bobby's dark one, she realised how much he would benefit from the company of other youngsters.

Chapter Two

Later in the evening Jan gratefully relaxed in Tom's reclining chair while Christine finished her last-minute packing. The children were in bed and Papa Kerr had retired to his room with a book, as had become his habit since his illness. Tom, himself, had offered to chauffeur Tim Greig to his home and Jan closed her eyes wearily, immensely glad to have a few minutes alone in the warmth and peace of the cosy little room.

The day's tensions caught up on her. She was totally unaware of the door swinging quietly open. For several seconds Mike Maxwell's green eyes surveyed her slender, long-limbed figure. He had forgotten how much taller Jan was than her sister. She was slimmer than he remembered too. Her hair had the same coppery brown sheen in the leaping firelight. His eyes dwelt on the faint blue shadows beneath the twin crescents of her thick eyelashes, now resting with childlike innocence against the delicate curve of her flushed cheeks. Her lovely wide eyes had always looked as though they had been set in place by a sooty, but exquisitely artistic finger—so clear and guileless. The teenage Jan had possessed no women's wiles. Why, oh why had he been fool enough to doubt her youthful innocence, even for those few minutes? His eyes moved instinctively to her soft lips, drooping slightly in relaxation. He wondered if she had any idea of the unspoken invitation of her full sensuous mouth.

His dark brows drew together in an impatient frown. He stepped closer, only to halt uncertainly in front of Jan's unconscious form. Her heavy lids lifted slowly.

'Good evening, Jan.' Mike's deep voice was very quiet, but Jan jumped as though she had been shot and her eyes widened in startled horror.

Mike drew in his breath at the dismay and instant panic he saw mirrored there.

'Wh...what do *you* want?' she gasped, clutching fearfully at the arms of her chair. His eyes narrowed slightly. They looked more green than grey and the golden flecks seemed to dance in the firelight.

Jan felt her heart thump erratically and her stomach muscles clenched as she observed the questing eyes, long powerful legs and the lean hard body that still shouted with masculinity. She closed her eyes and took a deep steadying breath.

'It has been a long time, Jan,' Mike spoke with his soft, Scottish burr. 'I have wondered about you—often. How have you been?'

Jan did not answer. A spasm, almost of

pain seemed to pass over her pale oval face, then she looked up—not at him—but through him. Her grey eyes were as cold as steel rapiers and her tone matched them.

'You may as well know right now—I would not have come to Shamlee—not even for Chris's sake—had I had any idea that you would still be here.'

Mike's eyes widened in surprise. 'But I have been back here six months—ever since William—Papa Kerr—became ill.'

'Yes,' Jan's voice was chillingly flat. 'Until this evening I thought you had returned to Canada as soon as he began to recover.' She shrugged her slim shoulders, assuming an air of nonchalance. 'Stupid of me I suppose, but no one mentioned your presence here.' It took all her willpower to control her thudding heart. 'Since Christine is depending on me—I must make the best of a distasteful situation. I trust that you will stay in your own house, and keep away from me—from here completely.'

Mike stared at her for several seconds in stony silence, trying to reconcile this cool, hard-voiced woman with the warm laughing girl he remembered. The warm appraisal in his eyes changed to a glare of cold disdain. When he spoke his words were clipped, his voice harsh.

'Then I am sorry to disappoint you Miss...' his eyes dwelt momentarily on her ringless fingers, 'Miss Carron. I shall be in complete charge here tomorrow, when Tom leaves. What is more I happen to live here—in case you have forgotten. I have regarded Shamlee as my home for the best part of thirty years. I have no intention of moving out to suit your little whims—even if the choice was entirely mine to make.'

Jan gasped incredulously and jumped to her feet as the full implication of his words penetrated. 'B...but you can't...I c...can't... We cannot both stay here! Not together—in the same house!' Her grey eyes were wide and accusing. She wondered if she imagined the fleeting shadow of disappointment before his eyes narrowed to glittering slits. His lip curled in contempt.

'It seems my early opinion of you was correct after all. You're a real peach! So soft and luscious on the outside—typically stone hard at the core! Nae doubt ye will have reasons of your ain for being so willing tae come!'

Jan stared back in silent consternation at the bitter scorn in his unwavering gaze. She remembered how thankful she had been to escape the empty desolation of Cherrytrees and the relief at leaving John behind. His clipped voice continued coldly, 'Unfortunately, circumstances make it necessary for us to share the same house. But I can assure you that even a frail old man and a couple of toddlers will be more than adequate chaperones as far as I'm concerned. I have not forgotten the kind of games YOU play!' His gaze travelled insolently over her slender body.

The colour which had drained from her face at sight of him now surged into her pale cheeks in a blaze of indignant anger. Games! How could *he*, Mike Maxwell, taunt her so? Her mind seethed in a futile search for a suitable scathing retort. But there were no words. For the first time in her life Jan resorted to violence with a resounding slap on his left cheek. The sharp sound of flesh on flesh shattered the silence. Jan gasped, horrified by her own incredible lack of control.

For one startled second Mike Maxwell stood like a statue. Then all the demons of the devil seemed to gather in his glittering eyes. His arm snaked out to grasp her in his merciless grip, forcing her to look at him, squeezing the breath out of her as he pulled her violently against his hard, lean frame. His mouth came down on hers with punishing force, bruising her tender lips against her clamped teeth until she tasted blood. The room began to spin and she clung frantically to his shoulders. Her mouth opened in a gasp for air but he gave no quarter. Indeed he seized his advantage to plunder the soft moistness with devastating, almost compulsive thoroughness.

Jan sagged against him helplessly and almost immediately Mike's own mouth softened. His lips began a tender exploration of the contours of her face down to the pulsing hollow of her throat. His hands moved over her spine, moulding her body to his. Jan knew his gentleness was far more dangerous than his violence as sensations tore through her—traitorous, unsought, unwanted emotions. Feelings she had thought dead, forgotten, were reawakened. She jerked her head away in a moan of protest but his mouth found hers unerringly, in a long sensuous kiss that demanded response. Jan felt the delicious weakness invade her limbs, the insistent throb of desire grip her body. Then sanity returned. She twisted her body in an effort to escape the drugging effect of Mike's kisses. 'Let me go! Oh please...' she pushed against his hard chest, as ineffectual as a moth against the window pane.

'What the hell's going on?' Tom's voice, harsh with shock, shook them both, and his eyes filled with dismay as he surveyed Jan's dishevelled appearance and bruised mouth.

'For God's sake, man, what's got into ye?'

Jan broke gratefully away from Mike's slackened grip. She pulled her sweater into place and nervously smoothed her tangled hair. She noticed Mike's heaving chest as he fought to regain control of his breathing. Tom shook his head in disbelief. Jan was incapable of speech. Her own reactions had shocked her as much as Mike's assault. She clasped her hands tightly together to stop them trembling and stared unseeingly at the patterned carpet.

The fire sputtered in the hearth—the only sound in the silent room. Tom moved impatiently to switch on the overhead light and they all blinked in the sudden brilliance. The spell was broken.

'Well Mike?' Tom's voice was calmer

now, but still astonished. Mike passed the back of his hand over his mouth and swallowed hard as he looked at Jan's bowed head.

'It will not happen again,' he said stiffly.

'I never thought it would have happened at all! God Mike, I believed you were the last man who would take advantage of...of,'

'Look I'm sorry you came in Tom!' Mike's mouth was a tight line, 'I lost my temper. I allowed myself to be provoked.'

'*You* were provoked? You know how much father wanted Jan here. He'll sense the tension between you immediately and he has enough on his mind without adding to his worries. I think I'd better call the whole thing off!'

Jan heard the frustration and disappointment in his voice. She saw Mike wince. She doubted if these two had ever had a serious quarrel in their lives. She knew they were close—closer than many real brothers ever were. She felt inexplicably guilty at the rift.

'Look man! You cannae do that!' Mike's tone was urgent. He knew too well how much this chance meant to Tom and to his family's future.

Tom stared at him, shaking his head wearily. 'Ach, I don't know. What is it with you two anyway?'

Jan tensed. She couldn't look at Mike.

'I give you my word, Tom,' Mike said quietly, 'I will not force my attentions where they are not wanted.'

'That's all very well,' Tom demurred, 'but I feel responsible for Jan. She is helping *us*.'

Jan gulped. Could she stand aside and let Tom miss his golden opportunity? Didn't she owe it to Chris? To all of them—to stay and to help?

'It...it's all right Tom.' Her voice was a croaky whisper. 'I...I... We've sorted things out between us n-now. You must go.' She heard Mike expel a long breath, and noted Tom's obvious relief.

'I think I'll go to bed now.' Tom nodded and gave her a grateful smile. But at the door her eyes were drawn to Mike and she gasped at the red imprint still lingering on his tanned cheek. 'He was provoked,' she admitted honestly. Tom's mouth twitched.

'Mmm well it makes a change from Mike's usual reception. Knowing you, Jan, he must have deserved it.'

Jan closed the door thankfully and leaned exhaustedly against the wall for a moment. It was long enough to hear Tom's reproachful, 'I would have thought you would be the last man to take advantage, Mike. Just because Jan has a child, it doesn't...'

'A child! She has a child?' Mike interrupted sharply.

'Bobby, yes. Surely you must have heard! I thought that was why you...'

'No! No I didna' ken! Bobby...? How old is he?'

Jan waited to hear no more. Her heart sank. Mike's opinion would be worse than ever now.

She had just climbed into bed when Chris came in and curled up on the end of the mattress as she used to do when they were children at Cherrytrees.

'Tom tells me you and Mike have had an argument already?'

Jan looked up sharply but it was clear from her sister's quizzical smile that Tom had kept the details to himself. 'Just a slight difference of opinion,' she mumbled.

'Mmm well I'm glad to hear it. I would hate to think of the pair of you quarrelling for the next six months but

I know how...prejudiced Mike can be, and how prickly you are about Bobby. I wouldn't want Papa Kerr to be upset by you two sniping at each other. Anyway it would be unsettling for the children.'

Jan was silent. William Kerr was as shrewd as ever. It would be awful if he were upset by the tension between herself and Mike.

'You and Mike seemed to get on so well when he stayed at Cherrytrees for the wedding,' Chris went on musingly. 'I remember Tom saying he had never known Mike to spend so much time in one girl's company before—except for Angela Dunbar of course. And mother told me he wrote to you at least twice afterwards. Yet you've always seemed to...to bristle at the mere mention of his name, Jan. I could imagine Mike being quite brutal in his criticism if he disapproved of you for any reason...but Tom says he didn't even know you had a child until tonight...I suppose it is a subject we instinctively avoided in Mike's presence...'

'Well Bobby is none of Mike's business!' Jan said more sharply than she had intended.

'Oh Jan,' Chris sighed anxiously, 'I...I

do hope you will forgive him if he says anything hurtful. You've always been such a clam about Bobby's father. It doesn't make it easy to explain to someone as prejudiced as Mike—that you are different I mean.'

Jan could not prevent a bitter laugh. Bobby's birth and the trauma surrounding it was not a topic she had ever discussed freely with anyone. Even her parents had not known the precise date of his expected arrival. When she had a nasty fall he had been precipitated into the world long before his time so they had never suspected the true identity of his father. Jan knew she would never forget Bobby's valiant struggle to survive, nor the dreadful worry she had caused her parents. At the time Christine had been expecting the twins and everyone had felt it wiser not to trouble her with details and uncertainties. Afterwards Bobby, himself, had become the focal point and delight of her parents' life as well as her own.

The events leading up to his birth, the pain and confusion, the tricky decision to operate—had been put behind them—if not forgotten. It was not a subject Jan chose to resurrect—even with Chris—and most especially not now with Mike Maxwell residing under the same roof as herself and Bobby.

She became aware of Chris's concern as she strove to find adequate excuses for Mike's attitude and opinions.

'His mother deserted him when he was just a child...and Angela Dunbar married his closest friend the minute she became pregnant. It is enough to make any man wary! But Mike has a tender heart under his dour exterior. He's super with the children although he can't possibly remember the loving example from his own parents. You will make allowances, Jan?' Chris pleaded anxiously.

Jan sighed. There was Tom lecturing Mike and Chris here defending him.

'I expect we'll get by. Don't worry Chris. Anyway Tom says Mike spends most of his free time with the Dunbars at Glenhead.'

Strangely the thought was not as pleasing as it ought to have been. 'I wonder why his mother ran away...?' she mused aloud.

'Papa Kerr once told me she was very impulsive,' Chris answered thoughtfully.

'Apparently Mike's father was over in Ireland when they met and they were married a few weeks later but I understand they were tremendously happy—right up until Mike was about three. She developed a severe kidney disease and the doctor warned Sandy Maxwell that she should not have any more children if he valued her life... From then on he treated her like a piece of delicate porcelain, according to Papa Kerr. Her own mother had died when she was born and her father—who was a very successful racehorse trainer—had indulged her every whim. Understandably she resented any restraints—even for her own good. She wanted another child. When Sandy Maxwell refused to take the risk she got it into her head that he had no more use for her. Her father died about that time too. I gather she alternated between bouts of depression and wild escapades. Suddenly she went off to America with a young Greek who had been camping on the Maxwell estate. Sandy Maxwell believed it was a temporary fling but he was desperately worried about her health. Eighteen months later he gave up hope of tracing her. He took pneumonia after a bad bout of 'flu but Papa Kerr reckoned he had lost the will to live—even for Mike...

'Tom told me that Mike inherited a substantial sum of money through a firm of Glasgow solicitors, when he was twenty-one. It had been in trust since his mother's death about seventeen years earlier. They couldn't tell him any details and of course the gesture came far, far too late to help Mike. He had grown up with her rejection, I suppose.' Chris shuddered. 'It's bad enough leaving the twins behind for six months—and at least I have Tom. Mike must have been devastated to lose both his parents so early in life. Can you blame him for being a little bitter?'

'No. It must have been dreadful,' Jan agreed, 'No wonder he thinks so much of Papa Kerr—and Tom.' She offered Chris a tentative smile and was rewarded by the look of relief on her sister's pretty round face.

Jan longed for the oblivion of sleep long after Chris had slipped quietly away to bed. She knew Chris had only told her Mike's history to win her sympathy—or at least a measure of understanding, but she couldn't get the picture of him as a little boy, forlorn and lonely, deserted by his mother,

42

all too soon to become an orphan, out of her mind. She remembered how bereft and bewildered Bobby had been, and indeed still was—by the sudden departure of her parents from his small circle of loving and familiar figures.

Had she been too hasty in her judgement of Mike? Too engulfed in her own confusion and humiliation? Certainly the women in his life had given him cause to be wary. Yet his behaviour when they had first met had given no indication of cynicism or distrust.

Her errant thoughts returned to the brief but wonderful time she had spent in his company. How young and naïve she must have been to give her untried heart so freely. Yet now John called her frigid. Was she destined to remain unmoved by all men except the one who had first awakened her innocent yearning and taught her to spin the most fragile dreams?

She had always been aware that the fires of her youthful passion smouldered on, but she had considered herself hardened and in control. Yet within minutes of meeting Mike Maxwell again every vestige of control had vanished. Even in anger he had fanned those smouldering embers into flames, sweeping away the defences which had proved so impregnable with everyone else.

It was five years since they had first met—in mid-September. The harvest had been finished early that year, and good too. Chris and Tom's wedding was a befitting celebration for two families whose entire lives revolved around farming. Everyone had joined in with gusto.

Tom, eager young bridegroom as he was, had insisted on travelling down to Cherrytrees two days before his great day—three eventful days before Jan's eighteenth birthday. His father and foster brother had accompanied him.

Chris had immediately whisked Tom off to see the vicar and thereafter disappeared. Jan was left to entertain Mike. In spite of the eight years difference in their ages she had felt completely at ease in his company from the beginning. Mike was keen to see around the farm, to inspect at leisure her father's pedigree dairy herd, and view the crops and countryside—so different from his native Scotland. Jan was delighted. For as long as she could remember she had been her father's shadow—the son he had never had. There was nothing she did not understand about the running of the farm, nothing she did not know about the different blood lines in their small, but well-bred, herd. Indeed farming was to be her chosen career, and she was already one year into her course at college.

Yet in spite of her competence and evident maturity, Jan was the first to admit that she was as innocent and inexperienced as a babe in arms when it came to relationships with the opposite sex. She had no shortage of boyfriends—but they were that and no more—partners for the local disco, chauffeurs to the Young Farmers' meetings.

Now, suddenly, she did not want this dark haired smiling Scot to realise that she was five years her sister's junior, in spite of her superior height and air of calm efficiency. For two long perfect days they shared an easy, happy companionship. It was the beginning of a sweet awakening for Jan and she revelled in every minute she spent in Mike's company.

On the morning of the wedding Jan went meekly with her mother and Christine to keep the appointment with the hairdresser and beautician—even agreeing to a complete re-style for her long chestnut hair. Chris was amazed and truly delighted with the transformation of her 'kid sister' into an exceedingly attractive young woman. Jan remembered how her mother's blue eyes had misted with happy tears at the sight of her daughters in their finery.

She had followed her father and sister down the aisle and found her own heart unexpectedly filled with a strange indefinable ache. Tom turned to smile at his radiant bride and his eyes shone with love. He was a resplendent figure in his swinging kilt and neat dark jacket with its silver buttons. Her glance moved to his taller, darker companion and she saw Mike's green eyes widen in appreciation at the sight of her own slender figure in the silk primrose dress. He smiled, warm, conspiratorial, binding them together with an invisible magic thread.

The little village church was full. It was a colourful scene, for the mellow sandstone walls and windowsills were hung with fruits and flowers of every description in readiness for the harvest thanksgiving service the following day. Voices lifted in harmony and Jan was surprised at the rich deep quality of Mike's as he sang with true enjoyment. To Jan the simple words of the wedding service and the atmosphere of abounding joy which filled their familiar little church were intensely moving.

They returned to Cherrytrees and the huge marquee which had been erected in the little paddock adjoining the orchard. The food was delicious and wine flowed freely. Robert Carron was determined that his daughter should have a day to remember. As the speeches and toasts and a great deal of laughter followed, Jan was conscious of Mike's presence, the deep voice, the rumble of his throaty chuckle. Her young heart grew wings and her stomach fluttered nervously.

Eventually the tables were cleared and the coloured fairy lights, suspended from the gnarled old apple trees, were lit as darkness fell. The band struck up a hauntingly dreamy waltz and Tom took his radiant bride proudly in his arms. After they had circled the floor Jan felt a light tap on her shoulder.

'Our turn at last,' Mike spoke softly, his arms wide in invitation. Suddenly Jan felt glued to the floor, overcome with nerves and shyness. 'Come awa' lassie, I willna' eat ye,' he murmured deliberately in his broadest Scots accent, his green eyes alight with laughter. Jan went into his arms for the first time, conscious of the eyes upon them, the cheers of the younger guests, the sighs of the older ones. She was grateful now for her mother's insistence on last winter's dancing lessons for there was no doubting Mike's expertise and enjoyment. He moved with lithe grace, his heavy kilt swinging rhythmically from his narrow hips as he led her round the almost empty floor. She gave a sigh of relief when they were joined by other couples and unconsciously relaxed against his broad chest. His arms tightened, holding her close and she felt strangely safe and protected.

'It was not really so bad, was it?' he smiled down into her eyes. Jan could smell the tang of his aftershave and the clean male scent of him. She felt her heartbeats quicken.

Even now, five eventful years later, she could feel her stomach muscles clench at the memory of the sensual pleasure she had known in his arms.

Mike had performed his duties towards the other guests meticulously, but he had returned again and again to her side.

Jan had been aware of the knowing glances exchanged by her parents and the affectionate twinkle in the eyes of William Kerr, Mike's own foster parent.

After a strenuous Gay Gordons, played especially for their Scottish guests, Jan had removed the bolero of her bridesmaid's dress. Only a few weeks earlier she had been youthfully self-conscious, considering the lightly-boned top and shoe-string straps far too sophisticated and revealing. She had silently vowed she would never wear it without the matching jacket.

William Kerr was enjoying his only son's wedding to the full and insisted on getting herself and Mike another glass of champagne. Sipping it and meeting Mike's enigmatic green eyes over the rim of the glass had been fun. How airily she had waved aside her mother's gentle warning about the effects on her unaccustomed system. But in her heart Jan knew, even now, that it had not been just the champagne which had made her familiar Cherrytrees seem like heaven.

Someone had asked Mike to sing. Jan remembered how much she had enjoyed listening to his lilting tenor voice—how proud she had been when the applause rang out amidst requests for more. He had made all their feet tap as he led them gaily through *Mairi's Wedding* with his kilt swinging in time to the music. He had chosen the last song himself and his gaze had sought hers across the crowded space as his deep voice rang with emotion.

But to see her, was to love her,
Love but her and love forever.

Jan felt her heart thud, filling her breast with a deep unfamiliar yearning as Mike's compelling green eyes held her in their spell. Now, as she had done so many times before, Jan recalled the rest of Robert Burns' famous song.

Had we never loved sae kindly,
Had we never loved sae blindly,
Never loved or never parted
We had ne'er been broken-hearted.

Jan turned restlessly in the big bed, thumping viciously at the pillows and longing for sleep to banish her most painful —and yet most precious—memories.

Chapter Three

Jan was reading a story to the children when Mike returned from seeing Chris and Tom off at the airport the following day. Three small heads clustered round the little book on her knee—eager to see the next picture and hear the adventures of Beatrix Potter's Jemima Puddle-duck. Bobby had heard it so many times he almost knew it off by heart as he saw the pictures. He never seemed to tire of it and always got excited at the first appearance of 'The foxy whiskered gentleman.'

Julie was the first to become aware of Mike's presence and silent scrutiny. 'Go way, Mike! Auntie Jan's reading us a story.' She waved her plump little arm imperiously.

Jan tensed. Her gaze flew apprehensively from Bobby to Mike. His eyes were fixed on Bobby's rapt expression and there was a startled look in his eyes.

'Read s'more!' Billy jumped up and down excitedly, then to Mike, ''S about

51

a bad fox an' a duck that's goin' to lay eggs!' His blue eyes were round with eager anticipation.

'Were you wanting anything...to eat? A cup of tea?' Jan asked uncertainly, unable to stand Mike's silent scrutiny any longer.

'Mmm? Oh I wouldn't mind a cup of tea before I start the milking.'

'No, no! Go 'way Mike!' Julie tried to shove him out of the doorway but he caught her up in his arms and tossed her small body lightly into the air until she squealed with delight. But Julie was nothing if not determined.

As soon as he set her on her feet she protested, 'We want to know what happened. Jemima has runned away to lay her eggs.'

Bobby stood apart, viewing Mike curiously and as soon as Mike had disposed of the wriggling Julie he crouched down to the children's level. 'And what is your name, eh?' he asked with the gentle, encouraging smile he had once given to Jan herself.

She held her breath. Bobby looked at her seeking reassurance. When she smiled and nodded, he moved closer to Mike. 'Bobby.' He offered his name shyly.

'Well hello, Bobby!' Mike held out his hand and gravely shook Bobby's small one. Bobby gave him his crookedly appealing grin and Jan knew he was won over. She hardly knew whether to feel relieved or sorry but she had to admit that Chris was right—Mike did have a way with the children. She thought of John, who at best was impatient and at his worst ignored Bobby altogether.

'I'se know what happened to Jemima,' Bobby told Mike now.

'You do?' Mike was suitably impressed. 'Will you tell us then, while...while Jan makes the tea?'

'S' my mummy!' Bobby said proudly, giving her his lopsided grin as he took the book from her knee to 'read' to Mike.

A little while later Mike followed her through to the kitchen, just as she was pouring boiling water into the teapot.

'He is a fine boy,' he said quietly but his eyes ran over her slender figure as though drawn by a magnet.

'Th...thank-you,' she muttered, feeling the ready colour mount her cheeks.

'Aren't you going to join me?' Mike nodded at the single place setting.

Jan shook her head. 'We had ours

earlier. Papa Kerr has gone to his room to escape the noise for a while.'

'Jan?' She paused on her way to the door, unable to hide the tension which Mike's proximity caused.

'Is there anything I should know—about Bobby?'

Jan stared back at him. What did he mean? Her face paled but with a tremendous effort she kept her voice steady and even summoned a nonchalant shrug. 'Not really—he's a normal, adventurous small boy,' Again she moved to the door.

Again he interrupted. 'And he is no concern of mine? Is that what you mean?'

'No. I mean yes.' She gulped in confusion. 'Did Chris and Tom get on the plane all right?'

Mike nodded and seemed to accept the change of subject but when she moved into the room he followed, carrying his cup of tea and a huge wedge of chocolate cake, much to her surprise and consternation.

Gradually she relaxed. He did not address her again but he evidently enjoyed the children's lively chatter.

The days seemed to fly. Jan was glad of the help of Christine's Mrs Monty, who came three mornings a week to help with the cleaning. In spite of the busy routine and constant cooking, baking and washing Jan felt strangely happy and almost at peace with her new life. The laughter and squabbles of three spirited youngsters and their grandfather's dry humour did much to relieve the tension between herself and Mike.

Julie and Billy attended the local playgroup two mornings each week in Westburn village hall. Bobby pleaded to be allowed to go too. Jan could not hide the doubt, sadness and reluctant agreement which chased each other over her expressive face. She hardly knew whether to be grateful or resentful when Mike offered to telephone Fiona Forsythe, the local organiser, on her behalf.

She was still standing gazing pensively through the kitchen window watching the children playing at their sandpit, when Mike returned from the phone. She was scarcely aware that her hands were still resting idly in the washing-up water until Mike pulled her gently away from the sink and wryly proferred the towel.

'Ye'll waste your hands, steeping them like that. And yes, Bobby can start this

Wednesday. Fiona would like to meet you though. She needs a few details—doctor's name, date of birth, that sort of thing.' He was standing very close and Jan felt the hard edge of the sink unit against her back. 'When is Bobby's birthday, Jan?' he asked quietly. Jan's head jerked up sharply. She stared back at those steady grey-green eyes in silence. 'When?' he persisted.

'What does it matter to you?' she stalled, trying to pass him.

One long, strong arm shot out, trapping her between him and the unit. 'I'm just interested—very interested as a matter of fact.'

'Oh you needn't worry,' Jan said calmly, deliberately misunderstanding his probing. 'He is older than the twins so he will be old enough to go.' Swiftly she dodged beneath his restraining arm, taking him unawares.

Bobby had actually been born several weeks prematurely in a haze of pain and confusion, after she had fallen down the steps of the milking parlour at Cherrytrees, but she had no intention of gratifying Mike Maxwell's curiosity on any matter concerning Bobby—not now—not ever!

The first morning after she had left Bobby in Fiona Forsythe's capable hands,

Jan could not help worrying. Would he make friends amongst so many strangers? Would the other children mock his Yorkshire accent? Would he remember to go to the toilet?

Mike seemed to sense her anxiety and lingered longer than usual over his morning coffee, telling her about two small pedigree calves which had been born the previous day and his hopes of one of them becoming a future stock-bull. It was only when he had returned to his work that Jan realised how easy it had been to talk to Mike again and knew that he had been offering silent sympathy.

Bobby of course had thoroughly enjoyed his new experience and Papa Kerr smiled at Jan's evident relief when they enjoyed a few quiet minutes together after lunch. 'Aye, he'll bring his share of sorrows, lassie,' he mused softly, 'they all do, but he'll bring his joys as weel.'

'Yes, I know,' Jan whispered sadly, thinking of her mother and the joy she had felt at seeing her daughters in their wedding finery, and later the blue eyes swimming with tears when she broke the news of her own folly.

Almost as though he read her thoughts,

Papa Kerr said gently, 'Your parents thought the world of Bobby. He gave them a lot of pleasure and a whole new incentive for your father—he was sure he would make a farmer some day.' Jan wondered if he had any idea of the provisions her father had made for Bobby's future, but the old man was shaking his head and reminiscing, 'Aye, aye an' mebbe he wis right at that... 'minds me o' Mike when he wis a youngster, does young Bobby—the way he cocks his heid at them wee calves and weighs 'em up. Aye he's a bright wee laddie.' He closed his eyes wearily, then suddenly opened them, fixing Jan with a piercing stare, but it was his words which took her by surprise.

'Ye hevna' met Mistress Angela McCall yet hev ye Jan?' He did not wait for her answer but went on, frowning, 'Her wee fellow, Jamie, has a look o' Bobby—especially they green eyes o' his. Aye!' He looked intently across at Jan. She felt her heart give a shocked tattoo. What was Papa Kerr suggesting? Why was he telling her there was a resemblance between her own small son and the son of Angela McCall—a woman she had never met? She looked warily at the old man but he closed his eyes again and she remained silent. But beneath that frail exterior she knew there was a shrewd and agile brain still.

Tim Greig had called in at Shamlee two or three times for a cup of coffee and a chat and Jan enjoyed his cheery manner and charm. In spite of his youthful looks and apparently light-hearted outlook on life, Papa Kerr assured her that he had the respect of almost every farmer in the district—at least as far as his work was concerned. His presence and knowledge were in great demand whenever the slightest complication arose.

One morning they were laughing together over one of Tim's amusing anecdotes when Mike came in. His face darkened into a frown and their laughter faded. Seemingly oblivious to his mood, Tim cheerfully informed him that he had got tickets for The Little Theatre for the Thursday performance. 'And I have persuaded Jan to come with me if you will baby-sit for her, old boy?' he added confidently.

'No, I will not baby-sit on Thursday,' Mike informed him quietly, his gaze steady and steely as he calmly regarded Tim's angry flush.

'You mean...You don't think I should

take Jan out? That's it isn't it? You don't *want* to co-operate!'

'Exactly.'

'Look man, even I can see that Jan is different,' Tim protested, 'There's a sort of...untouchable air about her—I just hope you have noticed it too!' he added grimly.

'Oh sure—I've noticed the "untouchable air"—as you put it.' He threw Jan a challenging glance and to her mortification she blushed furiously.

Tim looked from one to the other of them with a puzzled frown.

'I...er I will try and come with you some other time, Tim,' she hastened placatingly.

Tim's good-looking face broke into a smile again. 'Right! I shall hold you to that. You could always ask Mrs Monty to baby-sit. She often did it for Chris when Mike was in Canada.'

Jan nodded silently and watched him go. She was aware of Mike's disapproving frown and the tension in him. Why was he so opposed to her going out with Tim she wondered? Apart from his handsome looks and undoubted charm, there was a definite air of affluence about Tim Greig. Even today, in his working clothes, his tailored tweed jacket and fine worsted trousers spoke of quality. Any girl would be proud to be seen with him but what endeared him to Jan most of all was his love of animals and his patience with Bobby. Also she had no qualms about her ability to control Tim, should he try to step out of line, which was more than she could ever say in her dealings with Mike.

When Thursday evening arrived Mike did not go out and neither did he make any pretence of being busy with his book-keeping. He settled himself comfortably by the fire with a book while the rain beat heavily against the curtained windows. Jan frowned and went to tuck up the children. But when she had taken Papa Kerr his cocoa and medicine she felt strangely reluctant to join Mike in the cosy intimacy of the small firelit room. She pottered around the kitchen finding jobs to do, restless, but far from ready to go to bed.

Mike came to stand in the kitchen doorway, his finger marking the page of his book. 'For goodness' sake make us both a cup of coffee or something and come and sit down. You must be tired out, without prowling around in here!' His tone was brusque, almost angry, otherwise Jan knew she would not have obeyed so easily.

But she was no sooner settled down and opening the daily paper, when Mike closed his book with an ominous snap. 'Are you annoyed because you couldn't go out with Tim tonight?' he asked bluntly.

'No...not really. But you weren't very cooperative, considering you are evidently going to be at home anyway,' she told him tartly.

'It was for your own good. I've tried to tell you before, Tim is a wolf—and a fast one.'

Jan stared at him reproachfully. Her grey eyes were wide and clear, framed by a thick fringe of spikey dark lashes. Mike winced inwardly, knowing she was recalling his own speedy record. He pushed a frustrated hand through his brown hair and sighed.

'Tim has had every willing woman in the district since his...since... Och you're not that type!' he muttered in frustration.

'Aren't I?' The bitter irony of her tone was not lost on Mike.

'No! Damn it, no!' She was amazed at his vehement reaction. 'I've seen how

62

you are with Bobby, Jan. Anyone can see you love him. You're not the kind...you wouldn't just... Oh hell!'

Jan stared at him in surprise. Mike was rarely at a loss for words. But his next words were a worse surprise. 'Tell me about Bobby?' he pleaded and the dark shadows haunting his green eyes reminded her achingly of Bobby himself when he was unhappy and bewildered. She shivered. Mike in gentle guise was far more dangerous than Mike in a temper.

'There is nothing to tell.' She felt the agitation knotting in her chest. 'My life is my own now and I must choose my own friends and...'

'But Bobby? Surely I have a...?'

'No! You have Angela McCall—and her son—isn't that enough?' she interrupted on a note of desperation. 'Especially for a man who dislikes commitments.'

'Angela is different,' he declared impatiently. 'She's always been special—ever since I fought her first battle on the school bus. It is Bobby we're discussing. Who is his father, Jan?'

Jan rose swiftly to her feet, clutching her half-empty coffee cup.

'I'm tired. Good-night.

'But Jan...' Mike had risen too, 'I have a right.

'You have no rights!' Mike was blocking her path to the door but she tried to brush him aside.

'I'm not one of the twins, to be fobbed off as you please!' he muttered in frustration. Jan looked at his glowering face and unexpectedly found herself laughing.

'Well that's just what you look like—an angry small boy, sulking because he can't have all his own way.'

'Aah! But that's one thing I'm not, Jan—a small boy...'

Before she could guess his intention he had removed the coffee cup from her unresisting fingers and placed it on the desk behind her. Too late she glimpsed the light of challenge in his eyes. She tried to pass him but his arms encircled her—slowly, inevitably drawing her against the long length of his powerful body. She gasped.

'Mike! Let me go! Please, you promised Tom...' He was still for a moment, staring intently into her face. She knew he was aware of her ragged breathing and her treacherous heart thudding in response to his own.

'Yes, I promised,' he agreed softly. 'No forcing my attentions when they're not wanted. Are you sure they are so abhorrent?' Swiftly and unerringly, he bent his head to brush her lips in a disturbingly sensuous caress. Jan gasped at the gentleness of it and the emotions it triggered into life.

'Well?' he whispered against her lips. She turned her head aside, unable to protest, unwilling to assent, as his fingers explored the smooth curve of her cheek. He began to nibble her ear lobe, awakening a tumult of emotions before his lips moved on a voyage of exploration along her jaw. She turned her head in feeble protest and he found her mouth again. The very gentleness of his lingering kisses seemed to dissolve her resistance. She felt his arm tightening at her back, moulding her closer and closer to his lean hard body. Jan found herself clinging to him in trembling awareness as her fingers exultantly tangled in his hair. She was powerless to resist his tender assault yet some small part of her brain warred with the overpowering sensations he was arousing. She stirred in a faint, mute protest as his kisses deepened and his probing tongue explored the softness of her mouth. For a moment he raised his head to stare into her eyes as though he would penetrate her soul and its most secret thoughts.

'No...' she whispered beseechingly, but as his hand came up to clasp her wildly-beating heart his touch filled her with an almost unbearable weakness. She murmured his name helplessly against his searching lips.

'You're mine Jan—only mine...' he whispered hoarsely but with infinite tenderness. His mouth moved hypnotically over hers, drugging her senses. 'Tell me there was no one else, Jan.'

She wanted desperately to tell him the truth—that no other man could rouse her to such ecstasy...but the secret had been hers for so long now. The instinct of preservation was overwhelmingly strong.

'Please Mike, let me go. Let me think...' she implored softly. But his hands continued their sensuous caresses and his lips were against her mouth as he whispered, 'I want you, Jan—you and Bobby.' His voice was soft, gruff, pleading even. Jan wanted to surrender—to share the burden which had been hers—only hers for so long. Surely Mike would understand? Behind them the phone on the desk shrilled—then again—and again.

'The telephone...' she prompted huskily. Reluctantly Mike reached behind her, cradling her securely in his free arm, his eyes fixed intently on her face while the length of his body held her gently trapped against the desk. His voice was thick as he muttered the Shamlee number. She listened absently to the rumble of a voice on the other end—but within seconds Mike stiffened as though he had been electrocuted. His eyes widened in disbelief before his brows drew together in a dark menacing line. Jan's heart sank, even before he jerked angrily away from her.

'I do see!' he snapped coldly. 'She's right here,' he gave Jan a withering contemptuous glare, 'you can tell her yourself.' He handed her the receiver and strode swiftly out of the room without a backward glance. Jan shivered. One moment Mike was a tender, oh so persuasive lover—the next a stranger! How could she have forgotten his changeable moods? And she had come so close to trusting him! Never again must she allow him to lull her into such a false sense of security.

'Tim?' Her voice was sharp with disillusion. There was a pause.

'No it is not Tim. Who is Tim anyway?'

'John! I—I didn't expect to hear from you...'

'You know I care too much to let you slip out of my life so easily, Jan.' Johnathan replied in his usual smooth manner. Jan frowned. Did he really care or was the prospect of her father's money still bothering him? she wondered with unusual cynicism. Perhaps she should have told him that her father had intended Bobby to inherit Cherrytrees—another generation of Carrons. But John would have asked to see the will. He would have noted the codicil—added after her parents' holiday at Shamlee last summer. John would have given her no peace until he had ferreted out the name of Bobby's father—and made him pay... She shuddered at the prospect.

'I would like to see you, Jan.' John's plaintive voice interrupted her thoughts. Funny she had never noticed his whining tone before. 'I'll come up for the weekend. We'll spend it together—just the two of us...'

'You've forgotten the children, John. I can't leave them.'

'Oh Jan! Surely you must have some free time!' John retorted impatiently. 'I've some news for you. You will forget our little disagreement.' Jan sighed. John didn't understand children's needs at all.

'I suppose you could stay here, in Chris and Tom's room—if you're sure you really want to come. But I would have to check with Mr Kerr first.'

'Was that the old man who answered the phone? He sounded a bit stiff when I told him I wanted to speak to my fiancée.'

'John! You didn't! And I'm not!'

'Well we were just about engaged,' John answered petulantly 'And we shall be by the time next weekend is over and I've explained everything. I'll see you then, Jan. Good-night darling.'

Jan heard the click of the receiver and slowly replaced her own. She felt stunned by John's audacity and his arrogance.

The following morning Mrs Monty arrived as usual for her cleaning session and informed Jan that Angela McCall was spending some time in Edinburgh. Jan's face flamed with humiliation at the news. Now she knew why Mike had been content to spend so many evenings at Shamlee.

She shuddered, remembering. Obviously he had been amusing himself with her during Angela's absence. Testing her reactions—and how easily he had aroused her response. She offered a silent prayer for John's timely phone-call and vowed to give him all the attention he demanded on his visit.

Chapter Four

A brief ping at the doorbell followed by quick light footsteps and a gay, 'Hello!', heralded Angela McCall's arrival at Shamlee the morning after her return from Edinburgh.

Even in casual clothes she looked elegant. The slim fitting black skirt and bright red sweater emphasised her curvaceous figure. But it was not clothes which caught the eye so much as her vivid natural beauty and appealing smile.

Jan could see immediately, how a woman as striking as Angela would test any man's loyalty and her heart sank. Angela's features had the near perfection of a Botticelli painting and her flawless skin was the smooth texture of cream. Her thick black hair was drawn back in an old-fashioned clasp, revealing the graceful curve of her slender neck. Even in the dull light of a misty October morning it gleamed as blue-black as a raven's wing. Only her mouth was less than perfection, but, to a man of passion, Jan knew the full red lips would appear sensuous and desirable.

Angela seated herself with easy familiarity, on one of the tall kitchen stools, gently swinging one of her long shapely legs. The drooping lips lifted suddenly in a friendly smile. Her gaze was direct and the green eyes startlingly clear as she viewed Jan with frank curiosity.

'Would you like a cup of coffee? I was just about to make one.' Jan murmured awkwardly, feeling uncomfortably shabby in her faded jeans and cream shirt.

'Mmm that would be lovely, thanks, but I must not stay long. I really wanted to catch Mike. He is usually in for his coffee about this time.' She glanced down at the small gold watch on her slender wrist.

'Oh dear, you've just missed him!' Jan exclaimed. 'He has gone into Bayanloch for a valve for the milking parlour.'

'Oh.' Angela's voice was flat with disappointment. She shrugged, 'Oh well I suppose I shall have to wait until tonight then. I know Mike will be sure to come but I was just being impatient as usual!' She gave Jan a wry smile, showing small even white teeth.

Jan had expected to dislike Angela McCall on sight but in spite of her evident moodiness and possibly a stormy temper, there was something very appealing, almost sad about her as she sat gazing reflectively into the swirling brown coffee, which she was stirring absently round and round in her cup.

'You must be kept very busy,' Angela said, suddenly looking up with her disconcertingly penetrating eyes. 'I hear you have a little boy of your own as well as the twins?'

'Yes. But they have all been very good so far,' Jan answered her warily.

'Mmm, I suppose it's too much to hope you'll allow Jamie to keep coming down to Shamlee? Mike is so good with him and he just pesters to come.'

'We-ell, if you think he would still want...'

'Oh he would! Thank-you Jan. I may call you Jan?' But without waiting for a reply she rushed on, 'Jamie is so full of energy and endless questions. He is too much for my...my parents.'

Her voice shook ominously and Jan asked with quick sympathy, 'Is your mother keeping well? Chris told me she had had a serious operation.'

'Oh yes, thanks. Yes, she has made a better recovery than anyone dared to hope,' she murmured fervently. Then she shrugged her slim shoulders and her mouth took on its now familiar, sulky droop. 'It's just...well I was expecting great things from my trip to Edinburgh. But no one was any help to me! None at all! We are no further forward. Tell Mike to come as soon as he can tonight.'

Jan wondered if Angela was aware of her imperious manner. It was clear she was used to having her own way and did not take kindly to being thwarted in any way. What a strange mixture she was—almost a female version of Mike with his arrogance and his unexpected uncertainties.

As though sensing her speculations, Angela's eyes narrowed thoughtfully, then she took Jan completely by surprise with the spate of personal questions which seemed to burst from her lips. Jan blinked in astonishment and a flush of annoyance stole into her cheeks.

Angela saw it and sighed. 'I'm sorry! Really I didn't mean to upset you too. It's just...oh I'm so mixed up right now! But you must have been quite young when your son was born too. I thought perhaps...' She grimaced and her lovely face was shadowed, the full red lips drooped disconsolately as she returned her attention moodily to the swirling dregs of coffee in her cup.

'You know I was eighteen when Jamie was born and I thought I knew everything— or at least what I wanted and the best way to get it. I forced Jim to marry me! Now I wish with all my heart that I had been patient and let things take their natural course.'

Jan watched uneasily as a host of conflicting emotions chased each other over Angela McCall's beautiful, expressive face. Why was she confiding in her—a stranger?

'I was always impulsive!' she went on bitterly. 'But I don't know how I shall ever cope alone—as you have done.' Jan's head jerked up in surprise. Surely if she divorced her husband it would be to marry Mike? She would not be alone—unless of course

74

Mike reneged at the last moment. Had he already done so once before? She knew how much Mike feared the marriage trap which had indirectly caused his father's heart-break and subsequent death, as well as his own orphaned state.

She felt a surge of unexpected sympathy for the lovely young woman with her quick-silver temperament. Suddenly Angela jumped to her feet.

'Look at the time! I must go. Thanks for the coffee.' Jan blinked as she gazed after Angela's slim hurrying figure and listened to the impatient revving of a powerful engine.

No one could have doubted Mike's eagerness to reach Glenhead and see Angela again later that evening. He showered and changed in double quick time, refused to wait for his favourite cheese souffle and dashed off in his own sleek car instead of the slower Land Rover.

Tim had managed to get more tickets for the performance at The Little Theatre in a town about thirty miles away but for once Mike was too preoccupied to comment.

Later that evening as Jan wiped tears of laughter from her eyes she understood why the tickets were in such demand.

Although all the actors were amateurs the whole performance of the well-known comedy had been excellent, fresh and exhilarating.

Afterwards they reviewed the evening's entertainment over succulent steaks and crisp salads at one of the little town's few late-night eating places. Tim was clearly gratified by Jan's enjoyment but gradually he guided the conversation skillfully onto more personal topics. He already knew about the death of her parents and the subsequent sale of her beloved Cherrytrees but his own knowledge of farming and his genuine interest in her father's views and policies were reflected in his pertinent questions. He encouraged her to talk about her own work in the creamery laboratory, the hazards of trying to make cheese from milk containing antibiotics which had rendered the 'Starter' bacteria useless and her visits to the farmer culprits who supplied the milk.

'You know they always blame the vets for forgetting to tell them that their animals have been treated with antibiotics, don't you?' she teased Tim laughingly.

Tim grinned ruefully, 'We-ll we do our best to remember. I shall think of all the glamorous girls like you slaving away in the laboratories in future. That will remind me.'

He told her about his own work and how the practice had expanded since his grandfather started it. He was proud of the new clinic in which they could 'hospitalise' some of their patients. Suddenly his tone became serious as he tried to tell her how invaluable her own training would be to a vet's wife and how much Bobby would enjoy 'helping' with the animals.

Jan laughed lightly, trying to chivvy him out of his serious mood. 'Is this the line you shoot with every girl you take out?'

Tim stared back at her aghast.

'Not on your life! I've never considered the possibility of getting married...' There was a significant pause, then he added softly, wonderingly—'until now.' He frowned thoughtfully. 'You are so different some-how, Jan. I sensed it even on the train. Maybe it's because of Bobby. Perhaps one day you'll feel able to confide in me about him, for he's a fine wee boy. Any man would be proud of him. Even without Mike's warnings I could see you are not the kind to go for a cheap thrill,' he grinned suddenly, lightening the seriousness of the atmosphere, 'or to stand any hanky-panky from the Tim Greigs of this world.'

At the mention of Mike, Jan glanced furtively at her watch and gasped when she realised it was well after midnight.

As they drew up outside Shamlee, Tim turned towards her with his boyish grin, 'You will come out with me again Jan? After your Yorkshire friend has been? It has been the most stimulating evening I have had in a long time.'

'Yes, I would love to go with you again Tim. Thankyou for a lovely time.' Jan leaned forward and gave him a quick spontaneous kiss on his tanned cheek. She smiled at Tim's bemused expression and felt a rush of happiness at the prospect of their blossoming friendship.

She was surprised and more than a little annoyed when Mike appeared in the kitchen doorway. She wondered if she imagined the faint air of tension as his green eyes flicked rapidly over her.

'You certainly took your time at coming home, it's hours since the theatre closed.' He eyed her shrewdly. 'Still, you don't look too dishevelled, I suppose.'

Jan's grey eyes flashed angrily. 'Perhaps you should not judge everyone by your own standards! Tim was a perfect gentleman in spite of your insinuations. We had a thoroughly enjoyable evening!'

'So you are going out with him again. I suppose? "Will you come in to my parlour said the spider to the fly",' he mocked sarcastically.

'YOU should look to the ethics of your own conduct instead of listening to gossip about other people's,' Jan hissed furiously.

'Aah, but I don't need to listen to gossip. Tim makes no secret of his conquests—even boasts about them—though I suppose that's forgivable in his circumstances. As for you Jan, within a matter of weeks you are out with one man and inviting another for the weekend—to stay here, under the same roof—very conveniently! Then there is Bobby. It doesn't exactly add up to the picture of the quiet home-loving girl your parents painted!'

'My...my parents? When...?'

'They were here last year, when I was over on holiday. Mighty proud of you they were too—how well you had done at college, the excellent job you had carved out for yourself and the bonus the company had given you. They made no mention of Bobby though...'

'Because he is none of your business!' Jan snapped, but she could feel her heart racing frantically.

'Well I am not so sure! Sometimes when I watch him I wonder—some of his little mannerisms. A man gets a sixth sense about these things when he has no family to call his own you know. And if Bobby is my business then that makes you my business too, wouldn't you say?' His tone was soft—menacingly soft.

'Y...you're crazy!' Jan exclaimed. 'I told you before, we would not have come here if we had known you would be here too. Surely that proves we want nothing to do with you!'

'Aah but Bobby does! Now that he has had the chance to get to know me. We get on very well. There's a certain...rapport between us. I thought you had noticed?' he taunted grimly.

Jan had noticed. It was almost as though the two were drawn together by an invisible thread. As soon as Mike appeared, Bobby ran to show him his book, his toy, offer him his last mangled sweet from his sticky chubby hand. 'Oh yes!' Jan thought, 'I have noticed, but I shall never admit it.'

'You imagine things,' she scorned. 'All small boys like attention. It is your own conceit giving you an inflated ego again!'

She thought his face whitened but he had closed the distance between them in a couple of strides and she could only stare up at him with wide apprehensive eyes.

Suddenly he stretched out his arms, reaching unerringly inside the cream wool coat which she had draped loosely around her shoulders when she left Tim's car.

'I don't think you are as immune as you pretend either,' he muttered, his eyes holding hers hypnotically. 'Do you remember the night of Chris's wedding, Jan? How...'

'No!'

'How we danced in perfect harmony? How...?'

'NO! No, no!' Jan pushed urgently against his chest, but he merely tightened his arms, trapping her hands between their bodies and allowing her coat to slide from her shoulders to the floor. Briefly he stared at the neatly fitting brown and cream dress, that clung lovingly to her slender curves. Desire flared in his eyes. His mouth stifled her protest in a brief but totally devastating kiss before he released her abruptly and turned away—probably at the recollection of his reunion with Angela, Jan supposed bitterly.

'Go to bed! Damn it, go now! Before I really do something we regret...again.'

The last word was more of a strangled whisper, leaving Jan uncertain whether she had heard correctly or not.

Lying in bed later in the silent darkness, Jan re-lived those few moments in Mike's arms. The memories his kiss and his words invoked poured through the opened flood-gates of her mind with crystal clarity.

The feel of his muscular young arms, the steady beat of his heart against her teenage breasts as they danced, the final sip of champagne from the shared glass and then the laughter lighting Mike's green eyes until they too, danced with merry, gold-winged devils. Wordlessly they had moved as one, leaving the heat of the big marquee to dance hand-in-hand through the long cool grass of the orchard, beneath the swinging fairy lights and on into the deepening shadows of the old apple trees.

Gallantly he lifted her lightly over the stile, which only the previous day she had

82

vaulted like a young tom-boy. Side by side they leaned over the hump-backed bridge in companionable silence. The night was warm; music wafted in elfin notes on the faint evening breeze.

Even now Jan could remember how good it had felt just to be alive and in Mike's company. And even now she was still uncertain whether it had been the champagne or Mike himself stirring the very depths of her body and soul. It was quite beyond her to stifle the bitter-sweet memories of five years ago. Mike's finger tips traced a delicate pattern along the low line at the back of her silk gown, they turned by mutual consent and strolled along the bank of the little stream. Jan's feet were walking on air. If she stretched up her hand she could reach the moon and go for a sail around the heavens. She had laughed up at Mike, invitingly, unconsciously provocative. She heard his indrawn breath and skipped lightly away as he reached for her. He chuckled softly, following as she danced away along the familiar path, a slim pale wraith in the moonlight.

She stopped at the little wooden shelter where she and Chris had played as children.

It was a spot filled with happy memories. She sat on the sweet smelling hay bales and looked dreamily up at the huge harvest moon floating high and free in and out of the little puffs of cloud. Mike found her there and she beckoned him to sit by her side. As she turned to him the shining bell of her hair brushed his cheek. He put up a hand to brush it back, but his fingers trailed lingeringly down her neck, finding the hollow of her throat and the fluttering pulse there. Jan knew she would never forget the delicious thrill of his fingers with their slightly roughened tips as they tentatively explored the warm sensitive skin, where no man's hand had strayed before.

She trembled with the intensity of a deep unbidden yearning. 'Jan?' Mike's voice was husky. She knew he was going to kiss her. Her first real kiss, and she wanted it so much.

His lips were firm and cool but oh so gentle—almost reverent. She longed for more. Shyly her arms stole upwards, soft and warm and yielding against his face and neck. She felt Mike quiver, deepening his kiss as he sensed her pleasure. Her mouth, soft and innocent, opened obediently beneath his probing tongue. His arms tightened, moulding her closer and still closer to his hard body until she sighed with the sheer ecstasy of his caresses. She was intensely aware of Mike's husky whispers and knew that his joy equalled her own.

Wrapped in her dreamy haze, Jan made no protest when his lips tugged at the thin straps of her dress. But she gasped with trembling awareness as the cool night air met the warmth of her skin when Mike's fingers moved on a voyage of exploration which both terrified and delighted her. He lowered his head in a groan of desire and his kisses left a fiery trail which completely engulfed her.

Mike's arms cradled her, drawing her with him against the bed of soft hay. Any traces of frail resistance crumbled at his touch. It was almost as though the real Jan stood aside, waiting for the tumult of exquisite emotion to subside.

She heard Mike's deep sigh of pleasure, then his mouth sought hers again and again in a mounting frenzy of desire. Jan was aware only of the sweet ache of longing he aroused within her and her yearning to give herself wholly and completely. His voice, thick with emotion, whispered endearments against her fevered skin. Her limbs moved with a will of their own to obey Mike's whispered instructions before his mouth fastened on hers in a passion of ultimate possession.

She tried to speak but she was filled with the horror and panic of the real Jan Carron—the young, unsophisticated girl. She moved her head wildly, trying to obliterate the harsh reality of her own weakness.

'No! Please Mike...tell me...no...' she gasped incoherently between his now gentle kisses and crooning endearments.

'Hush my wee angel, hush,' he breathed softly against her hot cheeks as he rocked her against him, holding her protectively in his strong young arms. For a few minutes she lay still but tears of remorse squeezed beneath her tightly-screwed eyelids.

'Jan?' Mike's voice was soft, filled with concern.

'Let me go! Oh let me go!' her voice was harsh with rejection as she dragged herself hysterically from his arms. She ran from him, clutching the flimsy straps of her dress.

Neither of them were aware of William

Kerr enjoying a quiet smoke in the shadow of a gnarled old apple tree as they made their seperate ways back to the house—the one with such desperate haste, the other with dragging steps and a dejected droop to his usually proudly erect figure.

The following morning Jan was up early as usual. She was confused by her own thoughts. Remorse for her own weakness remained but in the clear light of a bright new day the poignant memory of Mike's kisses, his tenderness, remained. Gone was the innocent girl, but Jan knew that in her place there blossomed a woman. A woman in love! She did not know, but she felt the need for the perfect communion of mind as well as body, which she had shared with Mike. Her spirits soared with renewed hopes despite her conflicting thoughts. Mike would reassure her. They had discussed a multitude of topics since he arrived and their minds thought as one. He must have shared her ecstasy. He must! Surely something so pure and perfect could not be so wrong...?

Now in retrospect Jan realised just how naïve she had been. Her appreciation of womanhood had come too late. She had fled from Mike in blind panic and her rejection had been total—and devastatingly cruel. With the benefit of hindsight she knew Mike's own reactions would undoubtedly have been influenced by his parents' impulsive and youthful marriage and the heartbreak which had followed. Then he had been aware of Angela Dunbar's fickle heart and her own blatant admission of trapping his closest friend into marriage. Had Mike's anger and contempt been a shield for his bruised pride or had he truly believed that she, too, had tried to spring the marriage trap? She clearly recalled their confrontation on that sunny Sunday morning of her eighteenth birthday.

It was part of her morning routine to gather up the cows after her father had finished milking, and take them to their pasture. She knew Mike was already up and outside. Her father told her they had enjoyed an interesting discussion on the relative merits of various breed lines within his pedigree herd—amongst other topics. For once she had paid little attention.

Jan shoo-ed the cows along the lane. As always they moved at a snail's pace and she was pleased when Mike vaulted lightly over the fence and landed at the heels of a couple of the stragglers. He walked beside her in silence. Shyly she stole a look at his half-averted face. His set expression and tightly compressed lips shocked her. Gone was the easy companionship they had shared every moment of the last few days. She knew instinctively that he regretted the previous night's impulsive union as much—maybe even more—than she did herself and her heart contracted nervously. Unhappily she scuffed a loose stone with her toe and Mike broke the tense silence.

'I suppose there was no mistake. I did hear Tom and Chris wishing you a happy *eighteenth* birthday when they left?' he asked carefully.

'Yes,' Jan admitted in a whisper, staring hard at the dusty ground. Try as she would she could not control a guilty blush. Yet she had not lied about her age. He had never asked—but she knew he had assumed she was old enough to know her own mind—to make her own decisions. And she had been—until last night when her youth and inexperience had become so mortifyingly apparent.

She was aware of the eight years which separated them for the first time as she wondered what Mike expected from his women. He was twenty-six and she knew nothing of his experiences. Pride came to her aid and she lifted her head. 'What difference does age make to...to anything?'

He grimaced in disgust—but whether at himself or her—or even both of them, she could not tell.

'You are too young to know whether you are ready for serious commitment. You have so much of life ahead of you. How can you *know* that you are ready to settle down with one person for a whole lifetime?' Jan shivered miserably and looked at him askance, her grey eyes wide and bewildered. Her clear gaze seemed to stir him further. '*I* vowed I would never let *any* woman trap me into marriage. I was sure you were different—that we shared something unique...'

Jan stopped in her tracks, staring at him incredulously.

'S-settle down?' she faltered, sparing a cursory glance at the line of cows now ambling into their field before she faced Mike's frowning, stony-eyed countenance. He returned her stare but she thought his brow puckered uncertainly, then he went on stolidly,

'Your father has just been telling me of your plans for the future...' He gave a brittle, bitter laugh, 'How you intend to marry a farmer, like himself—preferably one who is as interested in breeding cattle too...' Jan waited. She had often spoken laughingly of such things to her father—usually telling him there was no one who could measure up to him if she was cajoling his support for something. But it was true she had never imagined a life that was any other way... Now she could only stare at Mike in disbelief as he went on relentlessly, 'He thinks I am the man you have "chosen"! God knows what he would think of your method of ensnaring a husband. He's such an honest, straightforward man himself. I suppose that's always something to be thankful for.' He gave a mirthless laugh and its harshness hurt. 'If I am to be coerced into marriage I can respect my father-in-law if not my wife!'

'M-marriage?' Jan could scarcely believe she had heard him correctly. She felt a hysterical desire to laugh. Coerced into marriage, ensnaring a husband... 'What do you mean?' she asked in a choked whisper.

'Oh come on Jan! You encouraged me very prettily last night, I admit it. But you see I know that's the way you young girls scheme, once you have set your mind on your man—it's the age-old marriage trap, I believe. While I, it seems, am just as foolish and gullible as the next man. I thought I had more than my share of restraint and self-control—until I was taken in by your clear, wide eyes and guileless looks! I thought you were the most wond...'

'You're despicable!' Jan never lost her temper. But now a slow furious anger welled up inside, swamping the sick, cold feeling in her stomach. Last night had obviously meant nothing to him. His tender caresses, the mystery and magic of budding love, the ecstasy of shared fullfilment... She had given innocently—everything she had to give—with no devious plans, no strings attached. Now the man to whom she had given so generously of her very soul, chose only to humiliate her. 'Y-you must be mad! As well as arrogant...a-and conceited!' she choked through gritted teeth. Mike snorted derisively. The slow fuse of her anger exploded, fuelled by his scorn and her own mortification.

'As I remember, Mike Maxwell—YOU needed *no* encouragement. I trusted you implicitly but I...'

'Trusted! Aah! now we have the con story. "I trusted you",' he mimicked sarcastically. 'I suppose that is the usual protestation of innocence!'

'Marriage to anyone has never entered my head!' Jan grated stonily, 'But if it ever does—YOU would be the last man I would consider! Goodness knows what interpretation your inflated ego put on my father's words—which were probably his idea of teasing anyway—but I doubt if he is eager to see me married off to anyone yet.'

She thought she saw a flicker of uncertainty in his eyes.

'Jan...' He took a step towards her but she shrugged away from him, hurt and angry.

'Just go away! Get back to Scotland. I don't *ever* want to see you again!' She no longer cared if she sounded childish. She began to run down the lane. He called her name with a new note of urgency and she ran faster until she was safely hidden by the banks of high hedges. Tears streamed down her face and she felt bruised in every

93

part of her mind and body.

Even now Jan could recall the utter desolation of that sunny Sunday morning—her eighteenth birthday and the end of her girlish dreams. She had lain face down, hiding her burning cheeks in the cool grass by the stream, hidden by the trailing willow branches, waiting until she was absolutely certain Mike would have left on his journey back to Shamlee.

Knowing so much more of Mike's own background and in the light of her own experiences, she could appreciate that he had perhaps had some justification for his hasty and cynical conclusions regarding her immature behaviour. Hadn't his own mother sown the seeds of doubt and uncertainty at an early stage? While Angela Dunbar had apparently been his first love since school days. But Angela had deserted him to pressurise his best friend into marriage—and that on her own admission.

As for herself, Jan knew she had been incredibly naïve. The possibility of pregnancy had not once crossed her mind. She shuddered at the memory of her dismay and the self-imposed isolation of mind and body until she had at last confided in her parents. Even they had never known the exact date of Bobby's expected birth and she had adamantly refused to divulge the identity of his father—to anyone.

Undoubtedly Robert and Annie Carron would have welcomed Mike as their son-in-law—even in the circumstances. They had liked and respected him. They would unwittingly have sprung the "marriage trap" which he both scorned and feared. And his own conscience and integrity would have made him an unwilling victim.

Chapter Five

Jan was amazed at Jamie McCall's intelligence the first time he came to Shamlee. His questions were endless and she could understand his grandparents being exhausted by his lively curiosity and boundless energy. But it was his engaging grin which arrested her attention and made her heart jerk alarmingly. The mischievous gleam which frequently lit his green eyes bore an uncanny resemblance to Bobby.

Even for his age though, Jamie was tall and more broadly built than Bobby. His creamy skin was very like Angela's except for the sprinkling of freckles over his nose. But to Jan's mind at least, there was a definite resemblance between the two boys. Mike too shared that same crookedly charming smile, maybe more mature, more cynical at times, but the same. Jan felt a feeling of nausea as she pondered the possible relationships.

The twins and Bobby followed wherever Jamie led. He was their hero and could do no wrong. They were no longer content to amuse themselves with toy tractors and sand heaps. Jamie had better ideas. They now pleaded to go to the barn to build a straw fort, to the cows' shed to swing on the innumerable gates, or to the calves' pens to play hide and seek. It was not so much that Jamie was unbiddable but that he was full of a spirit of adventure and he knew no fear.

Jan was relieved when Mike eventually took them off up the glen to count the sheep, while she concentrated on cooking their favourite lunch. Silently she admitted that Mike controlled them beautifully without so much as raising his voice.

The day before John was due to arrive, Tim proposed an unexpected outing including the children. It was a crisp October afternoon and Jan thoroughly enjoyed the drive along the narrow country roads. The hedges were bright with scarlet hips and the bronze and gold of autumn leaves. Here and there a mountain ash rose from the woody hillside, laden with ruby rowan berries glowing richly in the sun. The delicate leaves of silver-birch trembled like golden filigree against the clear pale blue of the sky.

Jan turned to Tim with shining eyes. 'This is a lovely surprise Tim. Thank you for bringing us.'

He grinned with pleasure.

'I'll remind you to show your appreciation later!' Then, more seriously, 'I must admit I enjoy my work even more on days like this. The countryside is especially beautiful just now. Do you think you could settle permanently up here, Jan? In Scotland?'

'If I found a job as interesting as the one I had, I suppose I might...' she answered carefully.

'Och Jan! You *know* I was not speaking of your employment prospects. I was sounding

97

out my own prospects—as if you didn't know!'

Jan was saved from replying by the children's impatient, 'When'll we see the puppies, Tim?'

He cast a rueful glance at Jan but he answered good humouredly, 'Not long now. But we have a wee package to deliver first...'

He swung the car off the road and followed a steep winding track up the hillside. At the top, exposed to all the elements, perched a small farmhouse with its gleaming white-washed buildings and solidly built house.

Tim jumped out to deliver a box of vaccine to prevent some young calves from getting an infectious cough and Jan gazed with awe at the view spread out before them. The fields were still fresh and green for there had been neither frosts nor harsh winds so far. Purple clouds of heather covered some of the steeper banks and down below, in the distance, she could see the silver gleam of the Solway Firth as it swept behind a fold of the Galloway Hills.

As soon as Tim returned, the children bombarded him with questions. Would the calves get sick? Did they have runny noses? How did he know if they got a sore tummy? And eventually, with mounting impatience—'How long now before we see the puppies?'

The puppies were the whole point of the outing as far as the children were concerned. Tim was giving routine injections at a small kennels and he knew the children would enjoy seeing a litter of golden labrador puppies. In an aside to Jan he murmured wickedly, 'It was the only excuse I could think of for seeing you again so soon!'

Jan returned his smile, 'Mmm, well I'm very glad you thought of it.'

Whatever his reputation, she decided she liked Tim Greig very much indeed. He was pleasant and uncomplicated—at least with her. No callous womaniser would have Tim's genuine love of children and animals. Briefly she thought of John, who had little time for either.

Jan smiled as the children fondled the pups with tenderness and pleasure, watched over by the good-natured bitch. The owner, Anita Reynolds, assured them that she was absolutely safe with children and one of the sweetest tempered animals she had ever owned. The puppies were beautiful with their plump, pale gold bodies and soft silken ears. It was difficult to get the children to leave them and only the promise of lemonade and chocolate biscuits lured them away.

'Can we see them 'nother day?' Bobby asked Mrs Reynolds earnestly, his eyes round with longing.

'Yes, of course you can. Perhaps your daddy will come too and buy one for your birthday.' She smiled, but she turned to Tim with a roguish wink, 'You know I never miss a chance and I would like to see the small one going to a nonbreeder.'

They stopped for the promised refreshments at a small cafe, looking out onto the choppy waters of a loch where the children could watch the coloured sails of some yachts dipping and swaying on the water. But their main topic of conversation remained the puppies.

'Can we really have the wee one, Tim?' Julie pleaded with her beguiling smile.

'Yes, yes I want a puppy!' Billy chimed in excitedly. Only Bobby remained silent, his small brows puckered in childish concentration.

'You will all need to ask Mike,' Tim

laughed lightly as he bundled them cheerfully into the car.

Back at Shamlee the children immediately regaled a smiling Papa Kerr with an account of their afternoon. 'An' the lady said maybe Daddy'd buy us a puppy...' Billy chirped breathlessly as Mike came into the kitchen to join them.

Again Jan noticed Bobby's unusual silence and the childish eyebrows drawn together in a bewildered frown which seemed to emphasise his resemblance to Mike.

'I'se want a puppy as well!' he announced suddenly, almost belligerently. He looked at Jan. 'Where is *my* daddy?'

Jan stared back at him dumbfounded. It was a question she had known he would ask one day—but to ask it *now*—and in front of Mike...

'We have to ask Mike! Tim said so!' Julie interrupted, and Jan could have hugged her niece for her timing.

But even as Bobby ran eagerly to Mike she caught the enigmatic gleam as his eyes met hers over her son's dark, rumpled head. She knew he would not let the matter rest. She watched nervously as he caught Bobby in his strong arms and threw him playfully in the air, making him chuckle merrily. Then he hooked one long leg around the kitchen stool and seated himself with Bobby perched on one knee, while Billy scrambled for the other.

'Now what's all this about buying a puppy?' he asked. Julie moved eagerly to his side.

'Can we have one? Please Mike...? Like Tim said, for our birfday?' she pleaded sweetly. Jan thought how hard it would be for any man to resist Julie if the promise of her early beauty and engaging personality matured.

'We-ell...' Mike grinned teasingly.

'Please! Please!' Billy yelled.

'Please, please,' Bobby echoed and Mike's face went still as he looked down into the smiling replica of his own.

'Is your birthday in July, Bobby? The same month as the twins?'

Jan caught her breath and glared at Mike, before she caught Papa Kerr's bright brown eyes moving quizzically between them. She gripped the shining steel towel bar on the Aga cooker behind her and watched helplessly as Bobby carefully folded down his small thumb and finger with his other chubby hand, proudly holding up three

102

small fingers for Mike to see.

'The third,' Mike nodded triumphantly. 'The third of July?'

'No's not July,' Bobby shook his head vigorously.

'No, of course not. The third of June,' Mike amended confidently. He gave Bobby an affectionate squeeze but he giggled and shook his head again.

'May? The third of May...?' The dark brows rose in silent query.

'No! Not May!' Bobby screamed hilariously, thoroughly enjoying Mike's guessing game. He was blissfully unaware of the electric atmosphere in the cosy kitchen. 'April!' he shouted.

'The third of April!' Mike echoed incredulously. 'It cannae be!'

But Bobby was bouncing up and down gleefully, chuckling with delight. 'Yes, yes that's my birfday. Isn't it mummy?' Two pairs of green eyes looked at Jan. Mike's were shocked. 'Can I get a puppy?' Bobby persisted impatiently. 'Please...?'

Mike brought his attention back to the three young, expectant faces with an obvious effort. 'They will be about ready to leave their mother by Christmas,' he said flatly, 'We'll see about one then maybe.'

The children danced around him, whooping with joy until Papa Kerr reminded them it was almost time for their favourite "cat and mouse" cartoon. They disappeared instantly into the small sittingroom and Jan knew it had been a deliberate ploy to get them out of the way.

She looked at Papa Kerr with wide troubled eyes and saw that his were filled with compassion as they moved from her to Mike and back again. Mike was sitting gazing dejectedly at the floor, his fore-arms resting on his thighs, hands clasped so tightly that the knuckles shone white.

Jan saw the sudden resolution on the old man's kindly face as he rose stiffly from his chair. He also enjoyed the cartoon film but as he passed Mike's bowed shoulders he paused and gripped his foster son firmly by the shoulder.

'Aye, aye laddie,' he murmured, and his tone was deceptively casual, 'Bobby is a fine, bright wee fellow. A son to be proud of. It's hard to believe he rushed into the world so early and had a struggle to survive, eh?'

Jan gasped audibly and Papa Kerr's brown eyes were apologetic as they looked into her startled grey ones. 'He knows', she thought. 'He knows Mike is Bobby's father! He wants Mike to know too... Why, oh why?' Her wide grey eyes moved anxiously to Mike. His broad shoulders no longer drooped. His green eyes were bright and alert, searching her face before moving questioningly to William Kerr—the man he regarded and trusted as his parent and his friend.

'Why was Bobby born prematurely?' he asked softly. Jan turned away from him, her hands clenching the steel bar on the cooker as though her life depended on it. She was incapable of speech.

'Jan slipped on the concrete steps into the milking parlour, at Cherrytrees,' Papa Kerr answered for her, adding pointedly—'It was in the middle of her course at college, you see, while she was doing her practical training...'

Jan must have made a small sound of protest for she heard him addressing her own rigid back.

'Your mother told me how it happened, when she was here last summer...' His voice was gentle, pleading for her understanding, and offering his in return. 'Aye,' he went on, 'they were proud of you, lassie, being sae brave an' all. *Nothing* mattered to them so long as you could walk again and that the bairnie should live and be all right.' She heard Mike utter an agonised groan. Then in the ensuing silence, Papa Kerr's slippered feet shuffled on the tiled floor and the click of the door told Jan he had left them alone. She trembled convulsively.

What had prompted her mother to discuss the trauma of Bobby's birth with Papa Kerr when they had obviously never thought of mentioning it, even to Chris—her own sister? Why had they exchanged confidences? Mike had been staying at Shamlee last summer. He had told her so himself. Had they noticed a resemblance? Was that the reason for her father's probing questions and unusual scrutiny on his return to Cherrytrees?

Mike's hands on her shoulders startled her, scattering her thoughts. She had not heard him rise and move silently towards her; now she waited tensely, expecting a tirade of angry recriminations.

'No wonder you never wanted to see me again, Jan.' The timbre of his voice was even deeper than usual and, surprisingly, it was far from steady. Jan swallowed hard, unable to turn and face him. She detected remorse—yes and regret—in his tone. It made her feel strangely trapped and she felt panic rising up in her. She could have met anger with anger, but...

'How you must hate me... And with reason!' Mike muttered almost to himself and his grip on her shoulders tightened, reflecting his inner turmoil. 'I know it is much...much too late—but please believe me Jan, I am sorry for what happened. Just one brief...'

'You don't *know* what happened!' Jan spun round swiftly, thoroughly agitated by his recollections, 'You don't know *anything*. You cannot be sure Bobby is your son—ever! You...'

'Aah, but I do know, Jan,' he interrupted with quiet conviction. 'You may have reason to be uncertain—though I doubt it. I could stake my life on your innocence at that time.'

'But you...' Jan began indignantly.

'Oh I know I said some hurtful things in the heat of the moment...but remember my pride had been badly bruised by your instant—your *total*—rejection. The moment I saw Bobby I knew he had to be my son...'

'No!' Jan denied, feeling the panic

107

welling in her chest, making it hard to breathe.

'Yes, Jan, yes,' Mike insisted, but gently. 'I looked into his eyes, held his hand in mine...I saw him smile. I *knew* he was mine—ours. Our son Jan. Yet I was almost afraid to hope...' He tilted her face to his and she saw the ragged emotion in his eyes. She knew she must harden her heart. He must never know.

'Even if you hate me,' he went on, speaking softly, 'at least let me help you—for Bobby's sake. I can give him so much...'

'He is well provided for!' she stated proudly.

'By your father?'

'Yes. He loved Bobby. He treated him as the son he never had. He left Cherrytrees to him...' Her voice shook, 'B-but he was too young. I couldn't keep it for him with some of the overdraft still to be paid. There was no one to run it. I had to sell it...I had to. But the money has been invested for him. He does not need you...' She knew her voice was wobbling out of control.

Mike's eyes narrowed thoughtfully.

'So...' he said slowly, 'If your father left Cherrytrees to Bobby...what about

108

you—and more important—what about Chris—your own sister? Are you allowing Bobby to deprive her of her rightful inheritance?'

Jan felt the colour drain from her face. He had unerringly touched her Achilles' heel. It was the one aspect of the whole affair which troubled her. In spite of the provision in the codicil—if Bobby's true father ever came forward to care for him—Chris had never once probed, pried or coaxed. She had been unstinting in her loyalty and support, thankful for her own good fortune in having Tom and the twins—but supposing anything were to happen to Tom...?

'Well Jan? I am right am I not? You are permitting Christine to make a big sacrifice—a sacrifice which is now unneccessary. Oh, it may not have seemed much when the money was tied up in Cherrytrees and cattle and there were loans and interests to pay—but now... It must have brought in a considerable sum. You *cannot* deprive your sister—and her children—for Bobby. You *must* let me help.'

'Never!' Jan stared up at him like a trapped rabbit—her grey eyes wide and filled with a nameless fear. Mike stared back at her and drew in his breath.

'You don't...you can't think I would try to take him from you!' He shook her, but gently. 'I would *never* part any wee laddie frae his ain mother! I know the effect of such partings only too well myself!' he muttered bitterly. 'Maybe that is why I have an instinct for my own kith and kin—especially Bobby. There has been a bond between us from the beginning. Such bonds are very precious to me. Let me acknowledge him as my son? Please Jan?'

Jan stared up at him uncertainly. He clearly cared deeply about Bobby's welfare—but he did not want Bobby's mother for his wife. How would Angela react to such a complication? Had Mike acknowledged Jamie as his son too? The thought brought a bitterness to her throat.

'Surely you should consider Angela first?'

'What do *you* know of Angela?' he demanded sharply, releasing his grip on her shoulders, and stepping back to peer into her face. It was his immediate reaction, the alert, almost defensive expression in his green eyes which destroyed her budding hope. It hardened her resolve never to give Mike power over herself and Bobby.

'You will never know whether Bobby is truly your son!' she gasped on a harsh sob, taking him unawares as she pushed past him in a bid to reach the privacy of her room. She needed time to think—to sort out her muddled thoughts—above all to decide what was best for Bobby's happiness and security. If she allowed Mike to acknowledge him, he would want to share Bobby's life, maybe interfere in his education—send him away to school perhaps? Certainly he would keep in contact wherever they went. Bobby would welcome him too. Could she bear it, loving Mike as she did? Yes loving him, she admitted bitterly. Could she go on seeing him, knowing that he loved Angela, and eventually as her husband, with Jamie and maybe other children? No! It was not possible. She must never admit Mike was Bobby's father. Without her word he had no proof. Surely without her cooperation he could do nothing?

Tomorrow John would arrive at Shamlee. If she had a husband and Bobby a father—surely then Mike must leave them alone?

Chapter Six

Johnathan arrived the following evening and with him came a chill autumn mist, embracing the glen in damp ghostly fingers. Jan's heart sank as he moaned about the inclement Scottish weather. She was relieved that Mike had already left for his usual visit to Glenhead.

Once the children were in bed Johnathan relaxed and mellowed in front of the blazing logfire in Chris's elegant drawing room—the use of which was a special concession to John's presence and one which she knew Mike would regard with contempt. Jan enjoyed listening to the news of her old colleagues and bit back a smile as John waxed almost lyrical in praise of Linda Wright. She had often felt sorry for her assistant when she had tried so hard to please John—knowing that even a crumb of praise from him had made her day. Yet often he had been so engrossed in his own affairs that he had scarcely been aware of Linda's presence.

Jan felt more than a little concerned for Vic Thomson though—both as her boss at the creamery and as a good friend. Apparently he had been warned by his doctors to take life more easily and he was at present trying hard to relax in the south of England for a few weeks. Jan sensed Johnathan's unease at his absence and for the first time since she had known him she heard him admit his own vulnerability.

'I just wish you had not been away at the same time, Jan,' he muttered worriedly. 'Next to Vic, you were the best at persuading the men to do what you wanted on the plant, and you know I am not so well up on these new installations as Vic Thomson. The firm are toying with the idea of setting him up as a part-time consultant for all their creameries in the north of England.'

Jan was relieved when John contented himself with a goodnight kiss and opted for an early night after his drive up to Scotland. She was even more relieved that the meeting between him and Mike had been postponed, at least until tomorrow.

Mike was amazingly cheerful as he accepted his plate of bacon and eggs at breakfast the

113

following morning. 'Oh, by the way, Jamie is coming down again today,' he announced blithely. Before Jan could hide her dismay, his eyes had caught her expression and she watched his lip curl in contempt.

'What's wrong, don't you like Jamie?'

'Of course I do! It...it's just that he...well the others are so much more difficult to manage when Jamie is around and...and with John here...I'

'Aah Johnathan! Of course!' he smiled mockingly and Jan wondered whether she had imagined the gleam of triumph in his green eyes before they were veiled by the sweep of his thick brown eyelashes. 'I take it he's not much use at helping to entertain adventurous small boys?' Then sharply, 'How does he get on with Bobby then?'

'All right,' Jan answered him reluctantly, for in fact the two seemed to ignore each other as though by mutual consent. She wondered suddenly whether Mike had invited Jamie intentionally—perhaps to try out John's patience. 'Did Jamie ask to come today?'

'Oh yes. Another of the male species succumbed to your fatal charms!' He glanced up and gave her a wry grin before returning his attention to spreading his toast thickly with the marmalade she had made earlier in the week.

Jan tensed as she heard John whistling tunelessly on his way down the stairs.

'Good morning, darling,' he greeted her cheerfully, but his look of surprised indignation, when he saw Mike tucking into his breakfast, was almost ludicrous.

'Umph! I did not realise you had to cater for the farm workers as well.' The condescension in his tone made Jan wince visibly and she dare not look at Mike as John continued, 'Surely your brother-in-law expects too much! Couldn't someone else feed him?'

He glanced disdainfully in Mike's general direction and a frown of irritation marred his handsome face. His pale gold hair was still damp from the shower and had been brushed sleekly back from his narrow forehead—the complete antithesis to Mike's dark, wind-blown curls. In his black polo-necked sweater and black trousers Johnathan resembled a well-groomed cat stalking around the kitchen. Although he was almost as tall as Mike and considerably narrower in build, he lacked Mike's lithe grace of movement and his air of leashed power. Beside Mike's dark masculinity, John appeared almost pretty and yet Jan knew well enough that women found him exceedingly attractive, and she had plenty of evidence that his desires were very much those of an active normal man. She gave herself a mental shake. She did not care for the conclusions her silent comparison had drawn.

Reluctantly she raised her eyes and the malevolent green glitter she encountered in Mike's had her performing belated introductions.

'You didn't say there was another couple living here, Jan!' John remarked, accusingly. 'Surely Mr er...surely his wife could look after the twins instead of asking you to absent yourself from your work?'

Jan looked helplessly at Mike and trembled inwardly at the sight of the sardonic smile twitching at the corners of his well-shaped mouth.

'I don't have a wife, *Mister* White,' he mocked deliberately. Jan's heart sank as she watched John draw himself up indignantly and puff out his narrow chest like a fighting cock but before he could voice his objections Mike added silkily, 'Of course I am hoping to remedy that shortly—once I get a few problems sorted out—you understand...?'

'Oh, er yes, yes.' John looked relieved by Mike's announcement and seated himself at the table to await his breakfast, but Jan felt curiously depressed by Mike's frank admission. Obviously his "problem" was waiting for Angela's divorce.

Almost as soon as Jamie arrived, the children disappeared outside and Jan's worries began.

She had just mixed the Yorkshire pudding batter and was separating egg whites in readyness for a baked Alaska when she heard furious wails and an indignant protest outside the door. Three little boys with soaking wet feet and trouser legs trailed into the kitchen leaving a path of muddy footprints, and with varying degrees of rage and anticipation on their small faces.

'Was 'is fault!' Bobby shrieked angrily, rubbing a muddy hand down his tear-stained face. Jamie watched expectantly, his green eyes round and bright. Billy stood hanging his head and peering at his twin for support. But Julie had other loyalties for the moment.

'Uncle John—he carried me over,' she boasted proudly. 'But they jumped and falled in.'

'Fell,' Jan corrected automatically. 'Fell in where?'

'Oh just a little stream—down by that clump of trees,' John muttered irritably.

'Whatever were you doing at the st...burn? You know it is out of bounds!'

'He said we could go!' Jamie accused gleefully.

'An' he sayed we's could go 'cross 'swell!' Bobby added sullenly.

Out of the corner of her eye Jan caught Mike's shadow and her heart sank. John began to bluster, blaming the children peevishly.

'Oh never mind!' Jan cut him short impatiently. 'Just help me get them out of these wet clothes and then I can get our lunch out. Jamie, whatever am I to do with you?' she pushed a flustered hand through already dishevelled hair, aware that her cheeks were pink and hot and that her nose was shiny, without the mocking appraisal which Mike chose to bestow on her as he entered the crowded kitchen.

John and Julie went smugly into the sittingroom leaving Mike to take charge of the three protesting little boys.

Lunch was delayed almost to the point of ruin but again it was Mike who came to the rescue, passing dishes and firmly doling out portions to the children, but Jan was aware of his enigmatic gaze following her every move. She knew that John had noticed Mike's keen attention too, even before those strong fingers of his rested provocatively at her waist on the pretext of reaching for the carving knife.

It was a relief when the meal was over and Papa Kerr led John and the children out of the kitchen, leaving her to clear up the debris. Surprisingly Mike elected to stay and busied himself stacking the dishes in the dish-washer while she dealt with the cooking pots. She wondered if he felt responsible for Jamie's presence and the morning's upheaval but as soon as the kitchen was restored to order she was left in no doubt about Mike's motives for staying behind to help.

His hands came down firmly on her shoulders and turned her to face him. 'He won't do, you know,' he said in a deceptively casual tone. 'Our Johnathan has no time for children and certainly not for Bobby.' His tone hardened. 'How can you associate with such a stuffed shirt?' Jan flushed and tried to move away but his grip tightened. 'How are you planning to entertain him for the rest of the weekend? What does he expect of you?'

'That's not your problem,' she told him firmly. 'But as a matter of fact we are going for a walk shortly.'

'I see,' he sighed and released her. Jan gave him a wary look and tossed her shining head defiantly. 'I will collect my anorak now and we'll get out of your way,' she told him sweetly.

'No. You can leave the bairns. I am going to be working on one of the tractors. I'll move it to the barn and they can play safely there while I keep an eye on them.'

'How mistaken can one be?' Jan thought later that afternoon.

John was pleased to have her to himself and they set off at a brisk pace over the fields and up the hill towards the boundary with Glenhead. Eventually they stopped for a rest and leaned against the fence, looking back down onto the rooftops of Shamlee, nestling like a doll's house in the fold of the glen.

'Jan?' John turned, and pulled her urgently, almost desperately into his arms. 'Jan, marry me! Now!'

Jan did not try to resist, indeed she hoped for the familiar surge of passionate response which Mike Maxwell could arouse so effortlessly in every quivering nerve of her body. She felt the quickening of John's breath and saw the flare of naked desire in his eyes as his arms tightened possessively. She closed her eyes, willing herself to return John's kisses, but even behind her closed eyelids she saw a pair of green eyes, gold-flecked with tender amusement.

It was at that particular moment that Mike, in his urgent need, scanned the glen with his powerful fieldglasses, an old policeman's whistle which was used only in emergencies, between his lips, ready to summon Jan's attention. The entwined figures were clearly visible through the binoculars. Mike would have given almost anything for the comfort of Jan's reassurance but the whistle fell from his lips to dangle uselessly on the string around his neck. He turned and ran swiftly back to the house and the fretful little boy who dazedly called in vain for his mother.

John pushed Jan away from him, eyes

glinting with frustrated anger. 'I don't do a damned thing for you, do I Jan? You respond like a block of ice! You showed more reaction to the touch of that...that farm-hand Maxwell!'

Jan tensed. She steadied herself with an effort. 'I...I'm sorry, John. But one's feelings can't be switched on and off at the flick of a switch,'

'I know that!' His tone was impatient. 'But you're so indifferent now! It's that business with mother and the house that's spoiled things for us, isn't it?'

'No! No I...'

'Well I've got news for you, Jan.' There was triumph in his voice. 'Mother has met an old army guy, retired colonel or something—plenty of money anyway, even for mother. She met him first at one of her bridge parties. If things work out as I'm expecting, they will probably marry soon and go to live at his place near Scarborough.'

Jan remained silent, biting her lip in dismay. In his way she knew John cared for her—but not with the all-consuming and gentle selfless love which she knew herself to be capable of giving and demanding in return.

She shook her head despondently. She would never have that love herself, but she could not marry John, feeling as she did.

'It's no use John. You must forget me. Please... Can we go back now?' She turned to retrace her steps but John caught her arm.

'You have changed. Even in the short time you have been up here. This morning, when I first saw Maxwell, I thought...well I almost thought he resembled your son, Bobby.' He laughed ruefully at himself. 'Of course that would be impossible, you'd only met him at your sister's wedding, you said. But it shows how insanely jealous I am I suppose. What about this man called Tim? Is he the man responsible?'

Jan breathed a sigh of relief. 'Tim is a vet. I do like him a lot,' she answered truthfully. 'But only in the same way as I like you John—as a friend—and he is very good with Bobby, and the twins too.'

'Umph!' John coloured guiltily and his tone was sullen. 'I expect I would be good with kids if they were my own. I suppose the truth is I have always been a bit jealous of your son, Jan.' He released her arm and they both turned to make their way back to Shamlee. 'I shall not give you up so easily, Jan. I shall return in a couple of weeks or so and hope you have come to your senses.'

Jan ignored the arrogance in his tone and tried to turn the conversation to lighter topics. 'Oh look,' she said with forced gaiety. 'Mike must have had visitors while we have been away. There is a blue car just disappearing round the bend of the road.'

As soon as they opened the door Julie ran to meet them, her blue eyes enormous and shadowed with fear. She snatched at Jan's hand to pull her into the small sittingroom and Jan recognised the sign of imminent tears in the soft trembling mouth and crumpled brow. Her own heart sank. 'What is it darling?' she asked softly.

'Billy's hurted! He...he...' She gulped back the tears with an obvious effort. 'He climbed the straw when Mike said "Nnno." He falled down. From up high...h...higher'n you.' She gave Jan no time to remove her anorak as she tugged her in the direction of the small room, trying hard to control her hiccoughing sobs. Jan felt the small hand tremble in her own. 'H...he w...wants Mummy.'

Jan knew the blood had drained from her face as she opened the door fearfully to find Mike kneeling beside Billy's prostrate form on the settee. She thought she saw a flash of relief in Mike's eyes before he lowered his dark head once more towards the white faced fretful child.

'What happened?' Jan asked quietly, aware of John standing disapprovingly behind her, a disgruntled frown marring his fair, handsome face.

Mike swallowed.

'He fell from a heap of straw bales—head first. The doctor has just left. He would have liked to speak to you, but you were—up the glen. Billy...knocked himself out for a moment or two.'

He raised troubled eyes to her face and Jan saw the deep anxiety in them. She moved to his side and knelt down, laying a cool soothing hand on Billy's brow. He whimpered softly. 'The doctor has checked him thoroughly, but he thought it would distress him unnecessarily to move him to hospital unless any further symptoms of injury develop. We have to waken him at regular intervals for the next twelve hours—to make sure there is no delayed concussion. Dr Armstrong promised to come at once if we were at all concerned, but apart from severe bruising, he thought he would be all right.'

'He should have sent the boy in for observation!' John stated arrogantly and Jan felt Julie's small hand clench. Mike pushed a distracted hand through his already rumpled hair. His own face was pale beneath the tan.

'I should have kept a closer check on them. They were having such fun too. I should have known...'

He sounded stricken. Jan had a sudden yearning to pull his head against her breast and comfort him. He looked so vulnerable, totally unlike the commanding, self-sufficient Mike they all knew.

'Don't blame yourself, Mike. If there had been any doubt in his mind the doctor would have admitted him to hospital. It is my guess you have probably had a worse shock than the children. I don't think there is any cause for alarm,' She tried to instill a cheery note into her voice, casting a meaning look at the children, and Julie in particular. Mike caught her meaning at once and rose to his feet. Julie's frantic grip relaxed and Jan gave her a reassuring smile.

'How about you helping Mike make a cup of tea for us all poppet? You are the only other lady about the house. I shall need you to help me until Billy is better.'

Julie brightened slightly and gave her a tear-filled wobbly smile as she nodded her fair head vigorously.

Mike gripped Jan's shoulder, almost painfully for a moment. 'Thank-you,' he said quietly. But as he turned to leave Jan remembered Papa Kerr and asked what had become of him. Mike's face shadowed immediately. 'He has gone to lie down—doctor's orders. He got er...upset.' Jan nodded silently and wished with all her heart that she had not gone off with John that afternoon.

John was inclined to be belligerent and to blame Mike's careless supervision for the accident. He had no concept of the behaviour of adventurous small boys. Mike remained silent, clearly reproaching himself and it was left to Jan to smooth things out. Mike refused to leave the house but John willingly volunteered to take Jamie home and it was a relief to Jan when he decided to stay a while at Glenhead, enjoying Angela's more congenial company.

Papa Kerr emerged from his room looking refreshed and after he had seen Billy sleeping peacefully on the settee the twinkle returned to his brown eyes. Mike heaved a heart-felt sigh and Jan realised then just how tense and anxious he had been about his foster parent as well as Billy.

Mike insisted that he should be the one to rouse Billy from sleep at the regular intervals the doctor had suggested, but shortly after one o'clock Jan was awakened from an uneasy doze by a single hoarse scream. She was out of bed instantly, running bare-footed to the children's room.

Billy had obviously been having a bad dream and was now whimpering piteously, 'I'se wants my Mummy. I want Mummy,' he sobbed turning his bruised cheek into Jan's breast as she cradled him in her arms, crooning words of comfort and stroking back his fair hair with gentle fingers.

Surprisingly Bobby and Julie had barely stirred and Jan was unaware of Mike's presence as he watched silently from the foot of the bed.

'Want a drink,' Billy murmured, moving his head fretfully from side to side.

'I will bring a glass of fruit juice,' Mike offered, but he came closer and knelt beside Jan to peer anxiously at Billy's purple temple. He looked haggard with worry and lack of sleep and Jan knew he was suffering far worse than her little nephew, who would almost certainly be bouncing around as usual by morning.

'I think he would be better in my bed,' she whispered. 'It would save everyone being disturbed.'

To her surprise Mike nodded agreement and the lines of fatigue relaxed in relief. 'I know he'll be safe in your care,' he said softly, 'I will carry him to your room.'

He slipped his arms between her body and Billy, lifting his small burden effortlessly but Jan felt the pressure of his hard, muscular arm through the thin muslin of her nightgown. It seemed to burn into her flesh like a fiery brand. She became embarrassingly conscious of her dishabille as she walked in front of Mike, knowing that the outline of her body must be clearly visible in the lamplight. She was also aware that Mike himself wore nothing beneath the dark blue terryrobe which barely reached his knees.

Billy began to whimper sleepily as Mike laid him on the bed.

He cuddled him close, rocking the boy soothingly. 'You get in beside him, Jan then I'll hand him over,' Mike suggested quietly. Jan was intensely aware of his brooding, unhappy eyes on her as she moved around the bed and climbed in.

She cuddled Billy's small body against her and she had a sudden crazy longing to do the same for Mike as he slowly relinquished his hold on the sleepy child. He bent to tuck the clothes around them both as though reluctant to leave them. Jan saw the tenderness and gratitude in his eyes and knew he would kiss her. They were not aware of John standing in her bedroom doorway, silently surveying the cosy scene with an ugly curl on his flaccid lips. His harsh tone shattered the moment of intimacy.

'So this is what happens while the old man sleeps soundly downstairs!' he sneered. 'No wonder you have no interest...'

'Wheesht man! Ye'll disturb him again!'

Mike muttered, straightening and indicating Billy's small fair head in the crook of Jan's arm. John looked momentarily surprised to see the sleeping child, then he scoffed sullenly,

'Umph! That may be your excuse for now but I knew there was something between you. The boy, Bobby, he's the im...'

'John!' Jan silenced him with an angry exclamation, but it was Mike who gained his attention.

'*You* had no ulterior motive in coming to Miss Carron's bedroom after midnight of course!' he bit out sarcastically. 'I suppose you always waken up smelling of after-shave and with your hair immaculate!'

Jan stared incredulously at John's sleek fair hair and the guilty colour staining his handsome face. His intentions were sickeningly obvious.

Mike turned to her with an icy glare. 'So now I know why you wanted him to stay here—conveniently in the next room!' Jan gasped and shut her eyes tightly, instinctively trying to shut out the sight of his bitter contempt as he went on scathingly, 'But for Billy you could have kept your torrid little assignation. You've finally convinced me! I don't suppose you are sure who fathered your son.'

'Get out! Get out of my room, both of you!'

She kept her eyes screwed tightly shut, trying to stifle the flood of gathering tears. She breathed a sob of relief as she heard the click of the door as it closed behind them.

It was dawn before Jan fell into an exhausted sleep and it was late before she and Billy appeared downstairs. Papa Kerr had supervised the children's dressing and Julie had importantly provided a breakfast of cereals and bread.

Of Mike there was no sign and John had already departed for Yorkshire, giving the unsettled weather as the reason for his early departure to a puzzled Papa Kerr.

Later that evening he telephoned Jan, contritely offering apologies for his appalling behaviour and his hasty departure. Again he pleaded jealousy as the cause and asked only that he be allowed to keep in touch. Wearily Jan agreed—too dispirited to care.

Mike had once more withdrawn behind a wall of moody silence.

Chapter Seven

Mike seemed to be out most evenings now and Jan scarcely knew whether she felt relieved or sorry. She knew he was co-producer with Fiona Forsythe, the play-group organiser, for the Westburn drama club. They were working on an evening's entertainment for the senior citizens' Christmas party. Angela had accepted the part of leading lady in a short sketch, clearly demonstrating her intention of remaining at Glenhead for some time yet. Jan tried not to listen for Mike's return but she knew he rarely came straight home from the rehearsals.

She found solace in Tim Greig's cheerful company, although he made no secret of his desire for a closer relationship with her. His open admiration did much for her morale, which had been at a low ebb since John's visit.

One crisp sunny day in November the children were looking forward to a visit to the swimming baths—another of the treats arranged by Tim as an excuse to see Jan on his afternoon off. They were to have tea on the way home at the lochside cafe and Jan was amazed at the children's eager anticipation.

So it was an awful anticlimax when Tim telephoned to cancel their plans just as they were finishing lunch. His father had cut his hand rather badly during morning surgery and Tim had to attend to his calls.

Looking at the three crestfallen young faces, Mike was moved to offer his own company instead, but not without a wary look at Jan. The children were ecstatic in spite of Mike's warning that he had to be back for the evening milking and there would be no time to stop for tea.

However a few hours later, after an hilarious and energetic spell in the well-equipped swimming baths, Julie at least chose to forget that particular warning.

'I'm terribly, awfully, hungry, Mike!' she announced hopefully, her blue eyes wide and ingenuous. Mike's eyes lifted to the sky and his eyebrows almost disappeared into his hair in a comically exaggerated prayer for deliverance from three rascals. Then he grinned down at them, relenting.

'Didn't I just know it!' he declared.

Much to Jan's relief Mike had almost returned to their former teasing friendship during the afternoon's capers and she made a tentative suggestion.

'How about fish and chips—eaten as we go along—no time wasted! Of course the driver will not want any...' she added innocently.

Mike shook his head in mock despair.

'You are worse than the bairns! Cruel with it too. You would starve a poor man to death.' He grinned boyishly and pulled in at the first open fish and chip shop. He dumped the delicious smelling package on Jan's lap and she felt her own enzymes begin to work overtime. 'And you will find a packet for me too,' Mike informed her as she carefully unrolled the wrappings. 'For your sins you can feed me as we go!'

By the time they were driving up the road to Shamlee everyone, including Mike, was replete. Jan licked her own fingers in childish delight. 'It is ages since I ate fish and chips like that or enjoyed anything so much,' she laughed ruefully.

'Mmm, me too,' Mike gave her an amused glance. 'And for once I resisted the temptation to bite the hand that fed me!'

'Only just!' Jan knew it was no accident

that he had frequently and provocatively possessed her fingers between his lips as she fed him while he drove slowly homeward along the quiet country roads.

The happy mood enveloped them all for the rest of the day and Papa Kerr beamed his approval at their happy laughter. The children were too tired to argue when bedtime arrived.

Mike showed no inclination to move from his armchair in the wee firelit room either, but eventually he stirred himself to coax Jan into lending him a hand with the book-keeping. She agreed willingly, happy that he was content to remain at Shamlee for this evening at least.

They spent a satisfying couple of hours working companionably side by side. At last Mike gathered up the pile of invoices and instructed Jan to put aside the book used for registering the birth of every pedigree female Friesian calf. She had volunteered to do this knowing what a finicky chore her father had always found it and knowing, too, that a hefty fine would be coming Mike's way if the birth registrations were not posted within the requisite thirty days. Mike was surprisingly grateful for her help and as she knelt to gather up the schedules she had been using, he smiled down into her face.

'See what a good partnership we could make, Jan—if we could forget the rest of the world and its problems,' he added almost bitterly.

'Well we can't—shut out the rest of the world I mean,' Jan retorted firmly, immediately thinking of Angela and Jamie McCall.

'We can, if we want to... Oh come on Jan! You know Bobby needs a father!' Jan drew in her breath sharply, but Mike went on relentlessly. 'And I need a wife. Surely you...'

'No!' her grey eyes dilated. 'No...no,' she whispered, knowing she could never marry Mike when he still loved Angela and knowing that Angela might yet become free to marry him. He would probably laugh her to scorn if he knew she loved him.

'Aah Jan, you'll be saying we are not compatible next and we have so many interests in common—apart from...Bobby.' Mention of Bobby made her nervous.

'Well we certainly quarrel easily enough! I don't think we are as compatible as you imagine.'

'No?' So softly spoken as he slid

137

gracefully to the floor beside her, scattering the papers she had just gathered together.

'N-no...' she whispered, leaning away from him, knowing she was trapped by the settee at her back, and even more surely trapped by his compelling green eyes so close to her own. His kiss was slow and deliberate, as though he sought to draw the very soul from her body. Her lips trembled and parted beneath his gentle torture. Desire flared in him but Jan knew she was far more afraid of her own response and the uninhibited passion which Mike could arouse so effortlessly in her.

'Please Mike...' she pleaded breathlessly.

He raised his head and looked down into her eyes as though he would search the inner recesses of her mind. 'What is it Jan? You *know* there has *always* been a certain spark between us... And I, fool that I am, I believed you were far too young for such a feeling to last! The first night I saw you again I knew it was there still—a certain chemistry. Don't tell me you don't recognise it too!' His hand moved swiftly to cup her breast. 'I can feel your heart racing like a startled bird. Your body betrays you, little one,' he murmured softly before his lips claimed hers again. Gently he lowered her to the floor, caressing her, murmuring endearments...

Jan was powerless to resist. Her mind rejoiced that he had put his black mood behind him and her body clamoured in response to his exploring fingers as he gently eased her blouse from the waistband of her skirt. He lowered his dark head to rain little kisses on the silken warmth of her skin, impatient at the obstruction of her bra. He lifted his head questioningly, staring hard into her eyes, then his mouth fastened on hers with a smothered groan. Exultantly Jan tangled her fingers in his thick thatch of unruly hair.

Mike moved restlessly. 'I need you Jan! I want you so very much.' His voice was muffled against her throat. 'And Bobby IS my son! Whatever foolish aberration I had during Johnathan White's visit, I'm sure he is mine. Soon...' He felt the sudden tension which made her slender body rigid beneath his hands.

He raised his head and stared in dismay at the horror on her face and the pain in her wide grey eyes with their fringe of dark curling lashes. She looked incredibly vulnerable and he hugged her into his arms protectively, but she began to struggle.

'Let me up! Let me go—please.'

He rose to his knees and helped her up onto the settee. She sat on the edge of the seat away from him. 'Jan, you cannae think I would...' She shook her head vigorously in silent protest.

Jan wondered how she could ever have forgotten Bobby—his birth—the circumstances leading up to it... Would she never learn? And there was Jamie too! And Angela—had Mike once whispered the same words to her? Did he still? She put her hands to her temples, pressing them, seeking to restore some order to her confused thoughts.

'What of Angela and Jamie?' she asked at last. 'Have you forgotten them Mike?'

He looked faintly surprised. Did he think she had not noticed Jamie's resemblance to himself and to Bobby? 'Would you expect to go on seeing them as you do now? If...if I...we m...married?'

Mike frowned and a wary look came into his clear green eyes before he turned from her. 'Of course,' he said at last, flatly, and his square jaw jutted defiantly.

'Then there is no more to say.' Jan rose swiftly and moved towards the door.

'Jan! Wait! You don't understand!'

'Good-night Mike,' she willed her voice not to tremble.

'No! Jan there are things you don't know, things I am not free to tell you!' He spoke urgently, almost angrily, as though he expected her to accept him unconditionally, whatever his past, present or future. In her heart she did not want to hear the words she dreaded—a confession that he was Jamie's father and that he still loved Angela if only she had been free.

'I think I can guess what you cannot say. Goodnight.' She closed the door firmly behind her, but she heard Mike's 'You can't! Damn it. You can't!' She was half-afraid he might follow her but she ran swiftly up the stairs and reached the sanctuary of her room with relief.

Jan twisted and turned restlessly when she eventually fell asleep. Her thoughts seemed to be waging a constant war with her feelings and she awoke unrefreshed to face the day's traumatic events.

The children had gone happily to play in the garden when she heard the clatter of a horse's steel-shod hooves on the flagstones outside. She gave a startled jump as the doorbell rang piercingly, long and loud through the house, causing Papa Kerr to mutter irritably.

Jan opened the door and jerked back in shock as she came face to face with the tossing head and prancing hooves of a big black stallion.

Angela was sitting nonchalantly on his back, magnificent in white perfectly tailored breeches and narrow waisted black jacket. Her own hair, curling beneath the hard hat, matched that of the gleaming black horse and her green eyes glowed with the same reckless defiance as her unpredictable mount.

'What a stupid thing to do!' Shock made Jan's voice high and sharp with anger. 'One of the children could have answered the door. You must take him away at once!' She looked anxiously towards the garden gate set in the corner of the small enclosed courtyard which Mike had told her was absolutely safe.

Angela was clearly in haughty mood and looked down disdainfully. 'Where's Mike?' she demanded imperiously.

'I don't know and I don't care! Just get that animal out of here.'

'You afraid of horses?'

'No. But I am afraid the children could come running out of that gate any minute and startle him. He looks a nervous, mettlesome beast.'

'Oh he's that all right.' She leaned forward to pat the arched gleaming neck and the horse threw up his great head, champing furiously at his bit and dancing impatiently on his long slender legs. At any other time Jan would have admired the immaculate grooming of both horse and rider and the magnificent picture they presented but she sensed the horse was uneasy in the confined space of four stone walls which allowed no escape for horse or human except through the narrow gate. Then out of the corner of her eye she saw the children slowly opening the garden gate, coming to investigate the noise. 'Go back! Please go back!' But she knew none of them had any fear of animals and especially one which could be ridden. She saw them hesitate and knew she must get Angela out.

'Look, there's Mike coming over the Wee Paddock. You can ride to meet him.'

'No thanks. I'll wait here.'

The garden gate began to open wider

143

and the horse seemed to sense the movement and skittered towards it. Jan grabbed his rein and began to lead him calmly towards the little gate, but she had not bargained for Angela's stubborn arrogance. The horse was halfway turned with less than a foot between his head and the stone wall. Jan concentrated on manoeuvering him carefully round about but Angela flicked her whip indignantly, involuntarily tightening the rein. The startled animal reared his head, flashing the whites of his devil's eyes, and trying to raise his forelegs. Jan was forced to release his bridle, but the children were by now thoroughly frightened and edging back to the garden gate. Bobby began to cry, sensing his mother's danger and the horse pranced madly at the unaccustomed sound. His hooves flailed the air once more and Jan cowered against the wall, squeezing her eyes tightly shut and stifling the scream which rose in her throat. Angela wheeled the horse sharply on his hind legs and his metal shod feet descended once more to terra firma—but not before one had grazed the length of Jan's thigh. After the first sharp, hot pain, Jan felt nothing but relief, as Angela expertly guided the prancing, excited animal through the narrow exit into the open yard beyond. She ran to the children and knelt to comfort Bobby, now sobbing loudly. None of them had heard Mike's running footsteps but they heard his harsh voice as he struggled to regain his breath.

'Of all the stupid crack-brained things to do! Grabbing the bridle of a horse with Nero's temperament! Are you mad?'

Jan spun round to confront Mike, his eyes narrowed to glittering slits and his face pale beneath his tan. Reaction was beginning to have its effect on her and her temper flared to match his own.

'Don't call me crack-brained. Any of the children could have been badly injured had they encountered him in such a confined area—killed even! You told me they were safe to come and go through here!

'Yes but surely you had the sense to see...'

'Sense! You tell your f...friend A...Angela about s...sense!'

Suddenly to her horror Jan burst into tears. She turned and ran towards the house but she saw Bobby's small face crumple in bewildered anxiety. 'Mummy!' For a second her flying feet slowed, then

145

she heard Mike's deep voice reassuring him, calming all three children and coaxing them back to their play in the garden.

Jan flung herself down onto her bed and sobbed, yet she had no idea why she wept so bitterly. True she would probably have one big nasty bruise and she had escaped serious injury by a hair's breadth, but her physical ills were as nothing. She did not hear Mike running up the stairs two at a time.

'Jan! Dear God you *were* hurt! I knew his feet came down perilously close to you!' He tried to turn her towards him, but she resisted, unwilling for him to see her tear-stained face.

'Go away! I'm all right,' she hiccoughed.

'Like hell you are!' He slid one arm determinedly beneath her and turned her gently to face him, stroking her hair away from her face with such tenderness that fresh tears gathered before Jan could control them. 'I'm sorry. I didn't mean to shout at you, Jan. It was the shock.' He shuddered. 'He could have killed you. Nero can be a brute. He is far too strong for Angela but she will not take advice from anyone just now. They are two of a kind—beautiful but wild and headstrong.'

Jan sniffed, fighting for control, wiping her cheeks with the back of her hand. Mike leaned forward. He smelled of animals and hay, as he reached for the box of tissues on the cabinet behind her. She winced fleetingly as his weight pressed against her thigh.

He saw her face as he straightened. 'He did catch you! Let me see, Jan.'

'No!' Then more calmly, 'It was just a graze. I'm all right. It didn't even tear my jeans.'

'He could have crushed your bone to nothing with those steel shoes. Let me see the damage.' His tone was gentle now and there was no doubting the concern in his green-gold eyes. Inexplicably Jan felt the tears well again in her eyes until she felt his hand tugging at the zip of her jeans. 'No Mike!' She pushed his hand away, 'It's only a bruise.'

'Mmm and a gey painful one I'd say. There's no need for false modesty between us, let me see now.' His tone was brisk and Jan knew there was no use arguing. Besides which she was beginning to feel horribly stiff. Mike's fingers moved impatiently to the stud of her jeans.

'I'll do it myself.' She stood up hurriedly,

147

but as she pushed the clinging jeans away from her limbs she was painfully conscious of the brief strip of pink silk she chose to call panties. But Mike's horrified gaze was on the purplish red flesh, already darkening in a broad angry weal from her hip down to her knee.

His fingers gently moved over the area and as they settled on her hip bone he exclaimed involuntarily, 'God you were lucky!'

Then to Jan's utter astonishment he clutched her to him and placed a brief hard kiss on her parted lips. 'Don't ever take such a risk again, Jan!' he muttered beneath his breath as he released her.

Jan bent to retrieve her jeans, completely confused by Mike's unexpected reactions.

'I have some liniment which would ease the pain,' Mike told her with a frown. 'But I think I should run you in to see Dr Armstrong.'

'I'll try the liniment,' Jan promised, 'But I am not going to the doctor.' Her mouth set in a determined line and Mike finally accepted her decision and brought her the white, evil-smelling lotion.

After a while Jan became aware of voices reaching her through the open window of her bedroom, which overlooked the small courtyard and a corner of the garden. She recognised Mike's resonant tones and guessed he must have been upbraiding Angela, though his voice was gentle as it reached Jan's ears. '...but I don't mean to "keep on at you", you must know that Angie. It could have caused a nasty accident though and how would you have felt then?'

'No worse than I feel now, I'm sure!' Jan recognised the bitterness and frustration, as well as a measure of childish defiance in the other girl's tone and guessed today's exhibition had been a form of release for her pent-up emotions. 'Anyway why didn't you turn up last night?' Angela went on petulantly. 'You know it is never the same when you are not there.'

'Angela, you *know* I have a lot of extras to attend while Tom is away.' he replied tiredly. 'Jan helped me with the book-keeping last night. She is very efficient...'

'Mmm I'll bet!' Angela retorted mockingly, but when she spoke again she sounded almost wistful and Jan knew she should close the window, but somehow she couldn't.

'Mike...are you interested in Jan? Sometimes I get the strangest feeling when I see Jamie and Bobby together... Oh I don't know!' She sighed heavily. 'I suppose it's all my imagination! I hardly know what I'm thinking or doing half the time these days.'

There was a brief electric silence. Jan found she was holding her breath, quite unable to drag herself away now. Mike's voice was quieter and very gentle,

'I know Angie. Things are difficult. I am beginning to appreciate how frustrated you feel,' his voice quickened on a note of urgency. 'You *must* tell Jim, Angie...'

'No! Please Mike, I can't! Not yet.

'Trust me. Let me explain to him if you can't do it yourself.'

'I-I can't... Not yet, Mike. If only I'd had some success with the people I saw in Edinburgh.' Jan detected desperation in Angela's tone as she went on, '*You* know how religious Jim's parents are. Rushing into marriage the way we did was bad enough.'

'Yes...well!' There was irony in Mike's tone. 'It seems to me you've paid for your impulsiveness recently. Anyway when a man really loves a woman...' His words were lost in the clatter of Nero's hooves.

'...if only I could be certain Jim would understand...' There was no mistaking the yearning in Angela's voice as Jan moved out of the bedroom where she had been rooted to the spot.

She felt drained and dejected. She had to put Mike out of her mind. There was no doubt he belonged to Angela and only Jim McCall and divorce stood in their way. She made a private resolve to keep Mike out of her thoughts and out of her life.

It was the decision to do something positive which finally made her accept Tim's repeated invitation to meet his parents a few mornings later. He had been attending a cow with milk fever. She had not responded well to the usual calcium and phosphorous treatment and Tim and Mike continued their discussion on possible deficiencies over a cup of coffee. As usual Tim seized the opportunity to persuade Jan to visit his home. This time, to Tim's amazed delight, she accepted.

Mike barely waited for Tim to leave before he burst out angrily, 'You cannot go, Jan! You are putting your head in a noose. Indeed you must find some excuse for a change of plans!'

'And what gives you the right to dictate to me, Mike Maxwell?' Jan felt the anger rising in her at Mike's arrogant and unreasonable attitude.

'Don't you know it is a *son* Tim wants? His parents too would be delighted with a grandson of Bobby's intelligence and his love of animals. It doesn't matter to them any more that he belongs to another man!' he added bitterly.

Jan stared at him and her face paled at his onslaught. 'Are you saying that Tim would never want me for myself alone? Is that it?'

'No! No I didn't say that!'

'You inferred it!'

'Has Tim told you about his accident?' Mike asked suddenly, quietly. A shadow passed over Jan's sensitive features but the pain in her wide grey eyes was for Tim. She nodded her head silently.

'And the result?' Mike persisted tensely.

'That the doctors are almost certain it will have rendered him infertile? Oh yes, he told me that. I also understand his reason for..."going wild"—Tim's own phrase. He hoped to prove them wrong.'

'I see,' Mike said at last and he seemed to have crumpled inwardly. There was no longer the light of battle in his green eyes. They were dull now, desolate almost and Jan wondered why. 'I did not realise things had gone so far between you and Tim.'

Chapter Eight

Jan enjoyed her evening with Tim's parents in the lovely old house which was both spacious and comfortable. Mrs Greig reminded her of her own kindly mum and by the end of the evening Jan wished with all her heart that she could wipe Mike Maxwell from her mind—and her heart—and love Tim as he surely deserved. It troubled her greatly to find that she was becoming more and more involved. She liked Tim too well to make use of him and yet she felt she was doing exactly that. If only they could find a solution to help them both. Could she have married Tim and learned to love him if Mike Maxwell had not reappeared in her life—if only he had stayed in Canada as she had expected.

Tim seemed content however, evidently considering their friendship was progressing now that he had persuaded her to meet his parents and gained their approval. After listening to the Greig family discussing local events Jan agreed to accompany Tim to the Lochan Farmers Ball, unaware that this was the main highlight of the district's social calender and that her acceptance, at least in Tim's eyes, was almost tantamount to announcing their engagement.

The significance of Tim's little strategy was not lost on Mike however and he did not hesitate to take full advantage of the cards which fate so obligingly dealt him.

Mrs Monty had just arrived to babysit on the evening of the Ball when the telephone rang. As Mike and Jan were still upstairs the motherly little woman dumped her overnight bag and answered the extension in the hall. Disturbed by Tim's message that he had to attend an operation, she quickly called for Jan. In seconds Jan had donned her robe and was running down the stairs, but Mike was already taking the receiver from Mrs Monty, clad in nothing more than a towel and still glistening from his shower. He ignored Jan's wild gesticulations and calmly informed Tim that he would give Jan a lift and pointedly replaced the receiver.

Apparently the young veterinary assistant who was on call was uncertain whether a calving heifer required a caesarian operation and Tim had gone to advise. He would need to stay if the operation was needed. Jan knew he could be delayed for most of the evening and she had no desire to be a superfluous third to Mike and Angela.

She turned angrily to Mike as he bounded back up the stairs.

'You had no right to interfere. I shall wait here until Tim can go too.' Mike allowed his eyes to travel slowly over her face, still flushed and shiny from her bath, down over the brief white towelling robe to her long bare legs and squirming toes.

'It makes sense for you to go with us. Dunstead Hall is far closer to Tim's than to here. We are saving him time and a journey.'

'I don't care. I'm not coming with you...'

Jan knew the words sounded childish and ungrateful in the face of a reasonable explanation and she saw Mike's mouth tighten.

'Get dressed, Jan. I'll be ready to leave in twenty minutes and I know how long it takes you women to preen your pretty feathers so you had better get on with it.'

Jan glared at Mike's strong muscular body resentfully. The towel was a sparse covering for his long limbs. Her eyes fell on the mat of springing dark hair covering his chest and her fingers curled convulsively. Everything about him shouted out virility. She felt the hot colour rush into her face as he returned her stare with an enigmatic look of his own.

'I said I'm not com...'

He swore softly as he stepped closer. The clean scent of soap mingled with after-shave and filled her nostrils. 'Will you dress yourself or do you want me to do it for you?' His fingers grasped her shoulders, crumpling the soft material of her robe and causing the loosely held fronts to gape even further. She made a hasty grab to pull them together but he gave an unrepentant grin.

'Let me go!' she hissed, 'And how about getting dressed yourself!'

He chuckled softly, 'Embarrassing you am I? How about lending each other a hand, eh? Though I daresay Tim would be here by the time we were finished!'

Jan struggled to escape his grip but it

was no use. 'I rather fancy helping you into those skimpy wisps you choose to call underwear.' Jan gasped. She knew he was enjoying tormenting her and she could do nothing to control the fiery blush which stained her face and neck.

Suddenly he lowered his dark damp head and she felt the touch of cool lips on the sensitive pulse at the base of her throat. He pushed her gently inside her bedroom door. 'That will do as a start for the evening,' he muttered wickedly. 'Don't forget—twenty minutes, or I shall be in to help.'

Jan knew he meant it too. Her fingers trembled as she tried to apply her make-up, knowing that she was going to need all the confidence and courage she could muster. She prayed that Tim would not be delayed too long and silently railed against Mike's arrogance in taking over arrangements.

At last she slipped her dress over her head, confident that it would not let her down. She had bought it while on a trip to London, attending a dairy conference with Linda Wright. It had cost the earth and but for Linda she would have reluctantly passed it by. Now she reached for the long zip which moulded the diagonal swathe of material into a bodice, revelling in the feel of the aquamarine silk against her skin. It was skilfully fashioned to emphasise her firm high breasts and slender waist, caressing one shoulder with a silken whisper while the other one was left alluringly bare, revealing the creamy perfection of her skin. The skirt clung lovingly to her narrow hips before swirling gracefully around her long legs. Her only jewellery was a chain of minute, graded gold ingots. Jan pirouetted before the cheval mirror and a tinge of excitement surged along her veins. The aquamarine eyeshadow, bought to match her dress, seemed to fill her wide grey eyes with mysterious shadows. Fortunately her hair needed little more than a thorough brushing to curve into a shining bell beneath her finely sculpted jaw.

There was a brief tap on her door followed immediately by Mike. Jan did not turn but she saw his eyes widen before they met her own in the mirror. For a moment he remained where he was then in two long strides he had closed the space between them. Jan turned slowly, tensely towards him. He lifted her hands and his green eyes moved appreciatively over her. 'You're very lovely,' he murmured softly, almost as though the words were spoken against his will. Jan's own eyes were wide and troubled, held by his compelling gaze. It was as though an electric current passed between them which could neither be broken nor ignored. Jan's hands trembled in his and his strong square fingers tightened and then released hers abruptly. 'We had better go.' He lifted her evening stole from the bed and placed it around her shoulders, but his hands lingered.

He bent to kiss her lightly in the tiny hollow beneath her ear and her stomach muscles clenched with an almost overwhelming desire. She wondered if Mike had any idea of his own magnetic power. He was virile to his finger tips and in the dark evening suit and pristine white shirt he glowed with a healthy cleanliness while every muscle seemed to vibrate with a leashed strength of its own.

The hotel had once been a mansion house and it was an impressive sight with its curving, tree-lined drive and pillared portico in the solid red sandstone of the locality.

Tim's parents were already there and

they greeted Jan with genuine warmth. But as they introduced her to their friends and some of Tim's she became a little alarmed by their proprietorial attitude and it did not help when Mike whispered mockingly. 'They seem to regard you as part of the family already.'

Although the meal took considerable time the dancing had begun before Tim managed to put in an appearance. He looked tired and strained. His attitude to Mike was almost belligerent when he claimed Jan as his partner. As the evening wore on she realised that his possessive manner had not gone unnoticed by other people and his sole monopoly of her began to irritate.

It was almost a relief when he led her out onto one of the small stone balconies outside the floor-length windows which were a feature of the beautiful ballroom.

'What a lovely place this is, Tim, and what magnificent chandeliers.'

Jan made an effort to lighten Tim's mood and steer clear of personal topics but she had reckoned without Tim's determination and for the first time in their acquaintance she became aware of a certain wild desperation in him. His arms moved around her in an iron clasp.

'Come on Jan,' he muttered against her averted cheek. 'Relax the ice-maiden image with me for once!' His mouth fastened on hers with bruising force. Another couple emerged through the long windows and Jan struggled in embarrassment, but Tim refused to release her as his mouth moved hungrily to her naked shoulder and back again to her neck.

'Tim, please!' she protested, 'I want to go back inside.'

'No! Not yet, Jan. I have to leave again soon.' His grip slackened a little and he gave a deep sigh. 'I promised to return to the farm in a couple of hours but I don't think there is much I can do. The calf was already dead and the heifer had been calving for too long.'

Tim was obviously upset. Jan felt a surge of sympathy for him. She knew how much he cared for the animals in his charge. He sensed the softening in her and pulled her close, kissing her as though he would draw strength from her. 'Marry me, Jan!' His voice was urgent. 'Just say yes. Please Jan!'

'Oh Tim...' Jan was filled with remorse. 'You know how much I care for you...but

I don't...love you.'

'But I love you enough for both of us!' he insisted, pulling her hard against him. 'Please Jan!'

'I...I can't, Tim. You...'

'Don't say no! At least promise you will think about it. Promise?'

'I...I...yes, but...' Her words were drowned by his passionate kiss. Jan wished with all her heart that she could give him the response he sought.

'This is our dance, I believe Jan,' Mike's deep voice startled them both. He was leaning nonchalantly against the window frame and Jan had no way of knowing how long he had been there or what he had overheard. She did know that she had never promised to dance with him, in fact it was almost a secret dread—to rekindle the bitter-sweet memory of dancing in Mike's arms again.

Tim released her slowly and asked Mike, with obvious reluctance, if he would see her safely home again. Jan wanted to protest but she knew it would be useless when she heard Mike reply.

'Yes. I intended to anyway. Your father told me you were going back to the heifer, Tim. I'm sorry about that. Angela has

162

already left with Colonel Baines. He is hoping to make a deal over Nero.'

Jan was surprised. She had seen Angela renewing old acquaintances and clearly enjoying her evening although she had scarcely danced with Mike, but she had not expected Angela would leave without them.

Mike stepped back into the ballroom, holding aside the heavy velvet curtain for her. Then she was moving into his arms, trembling as he guided her in time to the slow rhythm. It was nearing the end of the evening and as the floor became more crowded he drew her closer. They danced in silence and Jan wished the music would go on for ever, so sweet was the feel of his arms around her, his breath stirring the tendrils of hair at her temple. When the music stopped, he kept her in the curve of his arm. 'We may as well stay together now. This will be the last dance of the evening,' he murmured softly. Jan remained silent. How well Mike had timed his interruption and how neatly he had disposed of Tim. And yet she knew she was happy that he had.

The lights dimmed. The band began to play a haunting Scottish waltz and

Jan trembled as she turned into Mike's arms and gave herself up to the precious moments of pure delight.

'It is a long time since we danced together, Jan. Far too long for a man to be denied such exquisite pleasure,' he whispered softly against her ear. She felt his chin resting lightly on her hair and gave herself up to the pleasure of being in his arms, of his body moving with hers to the strains of the lovely haunting melody.

She could not stifle the faint sigh which escaped her lips as the music stopped at last. Mike too, seemed reluctant to break the spell which bound them. His fingers slowly trailed down her bare arm and their finger tips lingered and held together as he escorted her away from the cheerful throng.

In the car he tucked a light rug around her and switched on the cassette tape. The headlights cut a golden pathway through the night-dark, roads, cocooning them in a secret world of their own. The intimate tones of the country and western singer bound them in his spell.

Mike drove the car straight into the garage at Shamlee as the fine deep voice of the singer died away

Yes I'd rather love and loose you
Than never know your love at all.

Mike sang the last few lines softly, his own dark velvety tones echoing those of the singer—vibrant with some hidden emotion. Jan sat absolutely still in the close, warm darkness of the car.

'I can't see a thing,' she whispered at last into the waiting stillness, reluctant to break the spell which seemed to bind them, yet knowing that she should.

'I know,' Mike's voice came back, soft and husky, sending prickles along her nerve endings like a live electric current. 'But it doesn't stop us feeling—does it Jan?'

She knew he was going to kiss her—knew too that it had been inevitable since the moment they confronted each other on the upstairs landing earlier.

She did not resist when he slipped his arm beneath her shoulders, gathering her close to his fast-beating heart. His kiss was gentle, tantalisingly soft as his mouth traced the line of her lips and the curve of her jaw. Her frail defences crumbled as he caressed the sensitive hollow behind her ear and her hands moved unerringly inside his evening jacket, feeling the hardness of his chest and the soft thunder of his heart against her palm.

'Oh Mike...' she murmured huskily as his fingers trailed in a sensuous path along the sweeping line of her dress, pushing aside the folds of her stole so that his lips could follow in quick heart-stopping little kisses, until his mouth hardened and became urgent with desire. Jan returned his searching kisses in a rising crescendo of emotion. His hands roamed at will, caressing, exploring, drawing her closer and ever closer so that she felt the sinewy strength of him and knew that his desire equalled and surpassed her own.

'Oh Mike...' She heard her voice, husky in an agony of longing, as her arms moulded themselves to his body. He groaned as he buried his mouth in the warm hollow at her throat and she knew he ached with the same urgent longing as herself.

'Aah my little one... You...belong to me...' He punctuated his words with kisses, drugging her senses until she craved for more of him. 'God, Jan, I want you so!' His hungry mouth moved again to her own in a kiss that demanded her very soul. 'Just tell me you are mine—only mine... My own wee angel.'

Jan heard his impassioned whisper as in a dream—a dream that was a repetition of that other far-off hazy dream when she had been oh so innocent. Nothing had changed. Maybe she was the dark angel of his desire but Angela was the one who had his love. Yet still his touch, his kisses, aroused her to a frenzied passion.

'No!' Her voice was a hoarse, horrified whisper. 'Not again! Please not ever again!'

Mike drew back, startled by the sudden change, by the desperation in the protesting sob which rose to her lips.

Blindly, purely by instinct, Jan grasped the handle of the car door and thrust it open.

'Jan! Wait!' Mike's tone registered his dismay, but Jan ran towards the welcoming light of the porch and on with flying feet to the sanctuary of her bedroom.

She was appalled at her own weakness, at the ease with which Mike had taken her to the very pinnacle of desire and the brink of submission—again. How could she stay at Shamlee now? Should she take the children to the cottage she had kept at Cherrytrees? It needed cleaning, heating, carpets—all before she could organise the furniture she had stored. Who would look after Papa Kerr? Her tormented thoughts mingled into dreams that ended in nightmares.

The next morning Jan dropped the children at their playschool and returned to Shamlee with her troubled thoughts, Should she accept Tim's proposal of marriage—ask him to take her away immediately?

As she opened the door of Christine's little car, Mike appeared, effectively trapping her in her seat. His face was haggard and she guessed he had not slept too well either. He raised his hand, stilling the protest which had risen to her lips and his eyes were troubled as he regarded her pale face and fear-filled gaze.

'Please Jan—just listen for a minute. I had to catch you out here—alone. I...I am sorry I frightened you...last night. Believe me I did not mean to let things go so far...' He pushed a hand through his thick hair. 'Oh I meant to kiss you! All evening I had wanted to dance with you.'

'Mike!' Jan protested vehemently. 'I can't stay here...I...'

'That is what I wanted to speak to you about. Jan... You can't leave now. Things are going so well for Tom out there and you know they would come rushing back. Besides there is Uncle William...' Again he pushed a distraught hand into his tousled hair and his eyes held a haunted look. 'Jan this time I give you my word of honour that I will not jeopardise the happiness of three people by...by pestering you with my attentions. I promise that until Christine and Tom return I will treat you strictly as a friend. Will...will you stay...please?'

Jan looked up at him uncertainly and her own heart lurched with love and pain. Yet strangely she knew he meant to keep his promise. The happiness of three people, he had said. For Angela's sake she knew he would keep his word. Slowly she nodded her head, but in her heart she knew she had to smother her own love for him too—and it was going to be hard to live in the same house with him every day—to see him with Angela. But she had to do it—for Chris's sake she had to try. She owed her sister that—and more.

Suddenly she looked up at Mike with clear grey eyes. 'It will soon be Christmas. Are you going to get that puppy for the children!'

Mike's face broke into a smile of relief.

'You bet I am!' He turned and strode briskly towards the cattle sheds, and Jan watched his tall figure with an aching heart.

Strangely Jan felt calmer and more at ease with Mike than she had since her arrival at Shamlee. It was as though they had cleared the air between them and now they shared a real companionship, fostered by their mutual interest in the children. Farming and animals were an integral part of both their lives and Jan continued to help Mike with his book-keeping.

He spent a lot of his evenings at Glenhead or at the drama group practices in the village, rehearsing for the old people's Christmas party.

Jan knew they had drawn a curtain over their past but she recognised that it was a very fragile veil indeed. One which could be rent aside by no more than a look or the briefest contact. In spite of Mike's loyalty to Angela the situation between them was explosive.

Chris and Tom phoned from America to say they had plans for returning home soon after Christmas to discuss two items of important news. The twins were filled with excitement and anticipation but their joy served to emphasise Jamie's discontent. Angela's unhappiness seemed to have been communicated to her son, changing a mischievous child into a difficult and moody boy.

Tim was a frequent visitor, spending many of his free evenings at Shamlee. He had regained his usual good spirits, though he persisted in his efforts to persuade Jan to marry him.

Then suddenly their little world was transformed overnight by the first fall of snow—a transformation which was to far outlast the gently swirling snowflakes which had turned the fields and garden into a veritable fairyland.

At Mike's suggestion Jan dressed the children in their warmest clothes, and, unable to ignore the challenge in his laughing green eyes, she accompanied them all to the sloping fields at the back of Shamlee, towing Julie on a miniscule toboggan, while Mike pulled Bobby and Billy along on the large one he and Tom had once shared.

It was a joy to see their glowing young faces and hear their happy laughter ringing on the crisp still air. For Jan the scene recalled her own happy childhood, spent with Chris and their Yorkshire schoolfriends in the snowy fields at Cherrytrees. She felt a pang of regret for Jamie, missing such fun. He was probably snowed-up in the eerie that was Glenhead.

The thrill of the afternoon was a ride with Mike on his big toboggan from the very top of the hill. When each of the children had had a turn Mike turned an enquiring eye on Jan.

'No, no-thanks,' she murmured hurriedly.

'Chicken!' he teased with a glint of challenge in his eyes.

'Indeed I am not!' Jan denied indignantly, as he had known she would.

'Prove it!' He grinned boyishly, looking down at her pink cheeked face.

'All right I will,' Jan accepted the challenge with a proud toss of her head, but she cast him a wary look and her heart skipped a beat when she met his sparkling eyes and the familiar crooked grin. She felt strangely exhilarated as she watched the ripple of muscles on his jean-clad thighs as he climbed the steep slope with long easy strides, which she found difficult to match.

'Here old lady, you need a hand,' he teased, lazily extending his free arm. His whole body radiated with strength and controlled energy. His gentle humorous laughter was infectious and Jan felt a warm glow spread through her at their shared camaraderie. They were friends, sharing the joy of being alive and filled with health and youthful vigour.

At the top of the hill Mike settled himself onto the toboggan, making himself into a human armchair as he had done for the children and beckoned Jan to take her seat. She felt warm and secure, enfolded by his strong limbs, his broad chest at her back. His arms tightened. 'Comfortable?' he asked lightly, but she heard the faint huskiness in his deep voice and felt the warmth of his breath against her cool cheek.

'Mmm,' she nodded happily, and felt the slight rasp of his chin against her skin.

Below them the children played happily, engrossed in building a snowman. Mike made no move to set the toboggan on its way. 'Now I've got you where I want you,' he chuckled threateningly. 'There is no escape for you.'

'Oh I'm so frightened!' Jan relaxed

against him, laughter bubbling up in her. However briefly, she was once more in the arms of the man she loved. It was a moment of happiness she would cherish for the rest of her life—a cold clear winter's afternoon, filled with carefree laughter and the treasure of shared companionship.

'Ye're no ice-maiden and I'm certainly no frozen giant,' he murmured. 'We had better move,' But there was satisfaction in his tone, a determination in the heels that pushed the toboggan on its downward path. Jan knew she had never felt so free, so exhilaratingly alive, as they whizzed together through the rushing sparkling air, over the smooth white track, gathering momentum as they went. She had complete faith in Mike's ability to control and manoeuvre the toboggan so it was a shock to find herself floundering helplessly in a flurry of snow after Mike slewed them round so expertly to effect a halt at the bottom of the hill.

She looked up to see Mike still sitting safely astride the toboggan, one elbow resting nonchalantly on his knee, his hand cupping his face as he tried unsuccessfully to smother his laughter. His green eyes, perfect replicas of Bobby's were alight with mischief.

As she recovered from her astonishment, Jan glared at him. 'You did that on purpose! You wretch!'

The light of sweet revenge shone in her wide grey eyes as she blinked away the snow clinging to her long lashes. She scrambled swiftly to her feet, pelting him with a fistful of snow as she rose. Her aim was faultless and her speedy attack unexpected. Her laughter echoed on the still air as snow cascaded around Mike's defenceless head and she quickly followed up her advantage with several more snowy missiles until she glimpsed the merry devils dancing in Mike's eyes. She knew immediately that he would extract payment in full if he caught her. She took to her heels in flight, only to fall headlong over a tussock of rough grass hidden below the snowy mantle. In a flash Mike was upon her, sitting astride her prostrate body, holding her prisoner. He pulled her hands relentlessly from her laughing face and secured them above her head with one strong hand, while he gathered snow with his other. She screwed up her eyes and face awaiting her fate. But the expected rubbing with ice-cold snow did not materialise.

Cautiously she opened one eye and found Mike's face only inches from her own. She gazed transfixed as he allowed the snow to trickle from his fingers while his green eyes stared unwaveringly into hers, so close that she could see the golden irises and an expression of unbelievable tenderness. Slowly he traced the line of her glowing cheek with a faintly rough finger.

'I could think of a much more satisfying punishment than covering your face with snow,' he said softly.

He slipped his arms beneath her shoulders and pulled her into a sitting position hard against his chest, cradling her there, his chin resting lightly on top of her head. Sitting there in the snow, sheltered from the rising breeze and the view of their young charges, he held her in silence. They were no longer aware of the frost-filled air, the lowering clouds, the children's excited voices. They were oblivious to the world around them, closing in on them with its deepening shadows of uncertainty and despair.

'Jan...' Mike's voice was husky. 'That promise I made...I mean to keep it—though

God knows it's hard to do. Whenever I'm close to you there's temptation. As soon as Chris and Tom return we will...'

'Papa says come! Come an' phone Mike! Quick! Quick!' Julie panted breathlessly, standing on a grassy hillock, gazing down at them with her round blue eyes, filled with a mixture of amazement and anxiety.

It was a few seconds before her words penetrated the magic aura which surrounded Mike and Jan. 'Phone?' Mike repeated dazedly as the little girl persisted in her high-pitched excited voice.

Julie nodded vigorously as they scrambled to their feet. 'It's about Jamie. Papa's there...at the gate!' She pointed, conveying extreme urgency.

'Go Mike! Please go quickly!' Jan exhorted him anxiously. 'Papa Kerr ought not to be out in this weather!'

For one brief moment Mike's eyes lingered on her face and then he moved, running swiftly in spite of the snow. Jan watched his loping strides carrying him away and her heart was filled with a strange forboding which had nothing to do with the darkening sky and brooding, snow-filled clouds.

Jamie McCall was missing! No one knew where he had gone or why. Early that morning Angela had taken the Land Rover into Bayanloch for refills to their gas cylinders and a spare can of paraffin oil, afraid that the road to Glenhead would soon be blocked if the wind rose or if the forecast of more snow was correct. She had assumed that Jamie was still safely tucked up in bed but when she returned he was nowhere to be found.

Apparently he had been very upset the previous evening following a rare but stern reprimand from his grandfather. He had declared that nobody wanted him any more—even Jan had threatened to stop his visits to Shamlee. Yet Angela had still assumed he had found his way over the fields to Shamlee—too impatient to await her return, too stubborn to ask his grandfather for a lift. Now she was almost hysterical and blaming Jan and her own father for Jamie's disappearance.

Jan felt condemned before she had uttered a word when she encountered Mike's grave stare as he demanded an explanation. The sudden change in him made her nervous. Falteringly she explained how Jamie had entered the forbidden machinery shed and climbed onto the high platform of the combine-harvester, accidentally starting up the engine as he played with the controls. The shed had been filled with noise and fumes. Frightened, the other children had run to her, but Jamie had refused to descend from his lofty peak until Jan threatened to tell Mike himself and ban him from playing with the other children. Jan remembered how terrified she had felt but the mention of Mike's name had worked like magic and brought him down to earth. She had climbed up and switched off the engine.

Jamie had given a solemn promise not to go into the machinery shed again and Jan had assumed that the children had forgotten the incident. She could not believe that Jamie would run away from home on account of an incident which had happened a week ago. But when she looked at Mike she knew from his expression that he was not convinced. He was very pale beneath his weathered tan and already there were lines of strain and anxiety around his eyes and mouth.

Swiftly and in silence he began to assemble equipment to organise a search for Jamie. Already darkness was falling fast and according to Papa Kerr there were forecasts of more snow and blizzard conditions. Mike's jaw set.

'Then there's no time to lose.' He jotted down a list of names and handed it to Jan. 'These men will help. You telephone and ask them to meet at Glenhead.' Then he was gone without a glimmer of a smile or the briefest good-bye.

Chapter Nine

Darkness had long since fallen over the glen, the children were sleeping soundly and still there was no word of Jamie. Jan knew the search would be hampered by the gusting wind and frequent snow showers which had returned as daylight waned.

After the nine o'clock news Jamie's mischievous, freckled face was flashed up on the television screen with an appeal for information and a statement that the search was being suspended until daylight, as weather conditions were worsening.

Reluctantly Papa Kerr agreed to go to bed. Jan waited on. The hours passed but still Mike did not return. Tense, anxious, she had almost despaired of his return when he struggled into the back porch, stamping his numbed feet and shrugging out of his sodden garments. One look at his face told Jan there was no further news.

The doctor had sedated Angela and Mike had stayed at her side until she slept. He had returned to Shamlee, making one last search over the fields from Glenhead, hoping against hope for some sign that Jamie had passed that way.

Jan was wakened by the shrill ringing of the telephone and even as she jumped out of bed and pulled on her robe her taut nerves rebelled at the harsh summons. It was still dark and bitterly cold but Mike was already dressed, his face tired and haggard with worry. She watched his expression lighten briefly, then a deep shadow of distress once more darkened his strained features.

'Dear God, he cannae die! He cannae!' he whispered hoarsely at the inanimate instrument in his hand. Then, 'Aye, I'll be with you in a few minutes Angie. Hold on my dear, just hold on?' he urged tenderly. He replaced the receiver and turned to

Jan with such a stricken expression on his weary face that her own heart ached for him.

Automatically she moved towards the kitchen and shoved the kettle onto the hotplate. He followed, pulling on his anorak, checking his wallet and keys, while Jan made tea.

'I must leave...' he brushed aside her offer of food, his voice was grave, 'they have found Jamie. He had hidden in the Glenhead Land Rover yesterday morning. Apparently he hopped out when Angela stopped for paraffin. He wanted to get to his father. He...he hitched a lift with a couple of lorries.' Momentarily Mike closed his eyes, grimacing at the thought of the risks Jamie had taken. 'Fortunately the second driver has a family of his own. He thought Jamie had run away from school. When the weather deteriorated he phoned Jim McCall from a call-box. Jim met them with his pick-up truck at the cross-roads just as arranged. So when the man saw Jamie's picture on the television last night he phoned the police. They set up a search but they had almost given up hope of finding them. Jim's truck had skidded down a bank off the farm track. It is very remote...the—they had lain for a long time...' Mike's voice was gruff. 'Jamie is suffering from exposure. They think he will pull through. He's such a sturdy youngster... But Jim...is still unconscious. He lost a lot of blood from a head injury.' He clattered the cup into the saucer. 'They are moving him to Glasgow. I must get Angela there before...while there is still time.'

Jan's nerves were strained to screaming point when there was still no news by lunchtime the following day. The children were fretful, scarcely understanding the tension.

They all welcomed Tim when he appeared later that afternoon, stamping dirty grey slush from his boots.

'The telephone lines must be down,' he informed them. 'I have just taken a message up to Glenhead from Mike. Jamie is improving...' Tim's expression became grave, 'but Jim is still very ill. He did regain consciousness very briefly during the night and recognised Angela. She has refused to leave him apparently but the doctors think her presence will help as much as anything they can do.'

'Thank God!' Papa Kerr murmured

fervently and sank back in his chair.

'Now,' Tim beamed at the children. 'I have a pair of early lambs. They were born in the snow and they're real cute.' He grinned and turned to Jan as three small solemn faces brightened visibly. 'Mother invites you all to tea... It will relieve the tension for everyone,' he added hastily, anticipating Jan's refusal.

Jan only wanted to wait for Mike's return. But that could be several days yet. Obviously Angela was his first concern—and Jamie of course. Dick Monty was managing the milking and a man from the village had come to help with the snow clearing and thawing drinking troughs for the cattle. Yes, Mike would stay at Angela's side. The children were pleading eagerly to go to Tim's and even Papa Kerr seemed keen to get out of the house for a while.

Tim's mother welcomed them all with her usual warmth. She had prepared all the children's favourite things and clearly enjoyed their company. Bobby and the twins were thrilled to take turns at feeding the orphan lambs and while Tim attended to the evening surgery, Mr Greig brought Papa Kerr up to date with the local news.

The children explored a box of Tim's old

toys, lovingly preserved for the grandchildren Mrs Greig had once hoped to enjoy.

As Jan helped wash the dishes she became aware of the older woman's gentle probing into her relationship with Tim. She began to outline his bright prospects, inadvertently revealing her own dreams as well as those of her son. Jan was uncomfortably aware that she and Bobby were an integral part of their plans.

Gently she tried to explain that she had great respect and affection for Tim, but that she did not love him—could never love him—not as he deserved.

'Never Jan?' Mrs Greig queried faintly. 'Surely love can grow my dear?'

Jan shook her head sadly.

'Is it Bobby? You must know Tim would treat him as his own son. We would be proud to welcome him as our grandson.'

Jan felt brutal as she realised she must shatter the plans and dreams of Tim's kindly parents. 'It is not Bobby himself. I...I.'

'Aah! Bobby's father then? Did you love him so very much my dear?'

'I was too young to know what love really meant then—but yes I loved him—and I still do. I can never marry anyone else feeling as I do. Don't you see? It would be so unfair to Tim?' She willed the older woman to understand and forgive her.

'But after all this time... Surely you should think of your own future Jan? And Bobby's?' Mrs Greig pleaded helplessly. 'Couldn't you let Tim decide what is best? Perhaps you will see him in a different light...?' she tailed off hopefully.

'Please don't build your hopes on me, Mrs Greig. I know I shall always love Bobby's father—even though I can never marry him or belong to him. I value your opinion and your kindness too highly to be less than honest and I am too fond of Tim to cheat him by giving him only half of myself.'

Tim's mother tactfully changed the subject but Jan knew she had not given up hope.

It was dark and freezing again by the time they returned to Shamlee. Papa Kerr had enjoyed the change of company but he was tired and elected to go straight to bed. The children ran to find their night clothes and Jan hurried into the warmth of the kitchen.

As she flicked on the light Mike raised

186

his head from his folded arms, blinking dazedly in the sudden brilliance. There were deep shadows beneath his eyes and a dark stubble emphasised his lean jawline.

'Mike! You're home at last!' Jan made no effort to hide her joy and relief at his return. 'We had no idea you would be back.'

'No?' he muttered sceptically. Jan shivered as she took in the sardonic twist which curved his lips. His green eyes were cold and hard.

'You wouldna' waste much time waiting around for a man, would you Jan?' he sneered.

Jan stared at him aghast. They had heard nothing from him, and now... 'But we didn't...'

'Oh don't worry, I suppose you and Tim enjoyed your evening even if you did have to trail the whole family along. Anyway I get the message! I'm going to bed now that I know everyone is all right. When I saw the house in darkness and deserted I thought perhaps Uncle William...' He shrugged and his mouth twisted bitterly.

Jan was filled with remorse. It was unusual for Papa Kerr to go out at night in such cold weather. Mike would naturally be worried to find the house empty.

'Do you want a meal? A hot drink perhaps?' She faltered in the face of his brooding stare.

'No thanks. You have nothing to offer that *I* want apparently.'

The children came rushing back with their pyjamas and Jan turned hurriedly away to hide the rush of tears which blinded her. What had she done to deserve his cutting innuendo? They could not have known he would return tonight...unless...? Had he told Tim of his intentions? Had Tim planned his retaliation for Mike's disapproval and lack of co-operation? Or had he simply assumed that Mike's return would be unimportant to her?

Jim McCall was making good progress in the company of his wife and son. Jamie adamantly refused to leave his parents now that they were all reunited. His earlier defiance and reckless behaviour had been explained. According to his childish reasoning, if he had hurt himself during one of his escapades, then his father would have come to see him. Then Jamie had planned to confide how his mother cried at nights so often, how unhappy she was. The twins' excitement at the prospect of their parents' return and the approach of Christmas had emphasised his own insecurity and anxiety. When he saw the snow he had become afraid that his father would never reach them if he did not come soon. Then he saw his mother preparing to take the Land Rover into town. He had set off to find his father without further thought, and with a child's innocence and ignorance of the possible dangers.

Jan tried hard to join in the happiness and excitement as Christmas rapidly approached but beneath her serene smile her heart felt heavy. Whatever Mike felt privately, his relief at Jim McCall's recovery appeared to be genuine and he spent much of his spare time at Glenhead. Only with herself did he appear cool and aloof.

Jan began to fear she had imagined the warmth and friendship he had displayed when they had romped together in the snow as lightheartedly as the children.

True to his word Johnathan White had telephoned regularly since his fateful visit. Their conversations were friendly and uncomplicated by personal issues now. Jan looked forward to hearing of the latest developments at the creamery and

Vic Thomson's recovery. Linda Wright also figured largely in John's chats. But it was a surprise when he phoned soon after breakfast one morning. He sounded elated and after only a preliminary greeting he handed the telephone over to Linda.

Jan was sincerely delighted with her friend's news. Mrs White had married her wealthy widower and moved to Scarborough. John had put the house up for sale and received an excellent offer so he and Linda were planning to be married in February. Linda's only anxiety was Jan's own reaction to their plans. But the warmth of Jan's congratulations soon reassured her as well as her willing acceptance of their invitation to act as chief bridesmaid.

Jan was unaware of Mike's entrance as she happily discussed wedding plans.

'I may even return to Yorkshire before then,' she informed Linda, 'Chris and Tom are coming home the day after Christmas and I don't know what their plans are yet. But you know that nothing—absolutely nothing—will stop me getting to St Mark's at two-fifteen on February the fourth,' she promised.

A happy smile curved her lips as she

replaced the receiver and turned towards the door with a light-hearted skip. But her happiness for her friend died as she encountered Mike standing like a statue. His eyes were more grey than green in the cold morning light and they glinted like chips of rocky granite.

'Have you told Tim about your plans then?' he enquired with a meaning nod towards the telephone. His whole face seemed to register contempt.

'No, of course not! Not yet.' Jan stared back at him in surprise.

'Of course not!' he mimicked sarcastically, 'No! *You* prefer to keep *all* your men dangling on a string until you are sure you have hooked the one you want, don't you?' he grated bitterly.

Jan paled, bewildered and hurt by his taunt. 'Tim knows exactly where he stands,' she said defensively.

'Oh no he doesn't or he wouldn't keep coming back to you. I heard him ask—nay plead, with you to marry him. You've kept him dangling until "lover boy" came up to scratch!' he scorned.

Jan's colour flooded back into her pale face, stung by his incomprehensible recriminations.

'I don't know what you are getting at Mike Maxwell but I think *you* are contemptible. Just because the women in your life have not come up to *your* expectations and superior standards you think we are all fickle and disloyal! You are afraid of marriage yourself and you begrudge everyone else's happiness. Well let me inform you...some of us remain constant in our love for one man for a whole lifetime. And for your information, I am one of those women! God help me! My mother was! Christine is! But...but you are so weighed down by the great chip on your shoulder that you...you can't see any of us as we really are...you only *think* you want a woman when she is safely out of reach...' She rushed past him, trying to control the tears which sprang to her eyes.

Mike turned to stare after her retreating figure.

'So it has always been him!' he muttered grimly and left the house with an expression which boded ill for anyone crossing his path.

Suddenly Christmas was upon them but

even Santa's gifts and the longed-for puppy proved only a temporary diversion for the twins and their oft-repeated questions, 'How long now before Mummy and Daddy come home?'

The friendly little dog, with its shiny golden coat, received an ecstatic welcome from Bobby however and the two became instant and devoted companions. Mike had given his gift great thought and had included a small collar which he promised to have engraved when a suitable name had been chosen. There were also two brightly coloured bowls for fresh water and for the dog's own special food. Bobby was delighted.

In spite of Mike's contempt for herself, Jan knew he was unfailingly kind and patient with Bobby. She often saw him watching her small son with a tender, wistful smile which tugged at her heart-strings. She wondered how she would ever be able to part Bobby from his new pet and from Shamlee and all it had to offer.

At last the great day arrived. Mike had set out for the airport before the twins were out of bed and long before lunch Chris and Tom were greeting their children with a mixture of laughter and a few joyful tears.

After the celebration lunch which Jan had carefully planned, Tom had insisted that his wife should take a rest but Jan had a shrewd idea that it was more than jet-lag which prompted his concern for Chris. Later in the afternoon, over a quiet cup of tea Chris confirmed her suspicions that another baby Kerr was expected in the early summer. Jan knew the twins would be overjoyed at the prospect of another baby brother or sister and she was delighted for Chris and Tom, but she could not stifle the thought that this new development would have some bearing on her own immediate future and Bobby's.

The children went to bed early that evening, tired out after the day's excitement. Papa Kerr puffed contentedly at his pipe and looked happily round the circle of faces gathered before the cheery fire.

'Well Tom,' he said at last, 'What's yer news then laddie?'

Tom bit his lip but with a thoughtful frown he proceeded to tell them of the latest development in his career. His eyes flew constantly to his father's face and Jan realised how concerned he was for the old man's feelings.

He need not have worried. William Kerr had accepted his son's decision to follow an academic career with his usual stoicism and he was now inordinately pleased and proud of Tom's success. True, a shadow of regret flickered over his lined face when he realised that Tom's latest promotion meant extending his stay in America by another six months. Moreover Chris now insisted on taking the twins back with them at the end of the month. Most of the tours were over, Tom had been allocated a spacious house, complete with swimming pool, within easy reach of the research station where he would spend most of his time.

The news that the twins were leaving Shamlee jolted Jan out of her reverie. She would no longer be needed. She felt incredibly tired and dejected—so very much alone.

She caught Tom's thoughtful gaze.

'Perhaps you and Bobby will be able to stay on a while longer Jan. I know father enjoys your company and...'

Before he had finished speaking Mike interrupted abruptly, 'I'm afraid that is out of the question. We shall advertise for a housekeeper. Jan has already made her own plans to return to Yorkshire in February.'

Jan saw Tom's eyebrows rise in surprise but it was Chris who said, almost accusingly, 'You never mentioned returning so soon Jan! What had you planned to do with the twins if we had not decided to make a quick trip back as Mike requested in his last letter? No wonder he seemed anxious for us to come.'

Jan scarcely took in the implication of her sister's remark in her preoccupation with Mike's prompt rejection of her. She stood up and pretended to stifle a yawn, longing to be alone—to leave them all to discuss their plans for a glowing future while her own stretched ahead, bleak and empty.

'Jan?' Chris prompted sharply.

'Oh...I'm only going to Yorkshire to be Linda's bridesmaid. She and John are getting married in February. I would only have been away a couple of days. I could have taken the children if necessary. You should know I would never neglect them,' she said reproachfully.

She was totally unaware of Mike's start of surprise and the incredulity in the green eyes which lingered on the door long after she had left the room. Chris and Tom were amused and puzzled by Mike's unusual preoccupation as they discussed the legal and financial aspects of the transfer of Shamlee's ownership.

'Well I need my sleep,' Chris yawned at last. 'Especially if we are all invited to Angela's Hogmanay party tomorrow night, Mike?'

He gave a vague smile. 'What? Oh yes of course. Mrs Monty will baby-sit.' Then he added with unexpected fervency, 'I am glad you did manage to return so soon.'

Chris and Tom exchanged bewildered glances. Mike had shown a marked lack of enthusiasm in their earlier discussions, especially considering that ownership of Shamlee was supposed to be his heart's desire.

Jan had baked shortbread and made her first attempt at the traditional Scottish black bun—a rich fruitcake mixture encased in pastry for the New Year celebrations. Papa Kerr had hunted out his wife's old recipe book, eager to initiate Jan in the traditional Scottish customs. She had enjoyed leafing through the tattered, well-thumbed pages and looked forward to trying out some of the family's favourite recipes—the stovie tatties, clootie dumpling and Atholl Brose. Now she would never have the opportunity, she reflected miserably. Soon she and Bobby would be gone from Shamlee. She shuddered at the thought of breaking the news to Bobby. How would she tear him away from the little dog, now named Ted, after his favourite ginger teddybear? Had Mrs Greig been right after all? Should she consider Bobby's future before her own feelings? She knew Tim was looking forward to spending Hogmanay with her at Angela's party. She was sure he would try once again to change her mind and persuade her to marry him. She felt sick at the thought of belonging to anyone else but Mike. Yet Tim had gaiety and charm, kindness and consideration. Most women would jump at the chance of marrying Timothy Greig. She wished with all her heart that she could be one of them.

Jan was conscious of Mike's speculative gaze on her several times during lunch on that last day of the year. As soon as Chris had retired to her room to rest he returned to the kitchen. Jan could feel his green gaze boring into her back as she stacked away the clean dishes.

'Are you looking forward to your first Scottish Hogmanay, Jan?' he asked, taking her by surprise with the warmth of his tone after his swift rejection of the previous evening.

'Y-yes I think so. Tim says it will be fun. We are going "first footing" after the party.' She spoke with a gaiety she did not feel.

'Aah yes, Tim...'

Was it her imagination or had his expression hardened at the mention of Tim? She shook her head sadly as Mike turned on his heel and left the kitchen abruptly. She would never understand Mike's complex nature.

Immediately after he had finished the evening milking Mike changed into clean jeans and announced his intention of going out for a while. There was a determined thrust to his lean jaw. In spite of Chris's protest that it would soon be time to dress for Angela's party, he strode swiftly out to his car, completely ignoring Tom's startled query.

Chapter Ten

Jim McCall rose to greet them from the depths of a blue velvet chair in the Dunbars' large, elegantly furnished lounge. Jan liked the grip of his hand and the shrewd but kindly hazel eyes surrounded by a myriad of tiny lines. She could imagine him scanning the hills and glens of his native Highlands with deep contentment. In spite of his recent illness and a bandaged head he still bore the look of an outdoor man. His hair was a gingery brown but the set of his head and his broad shoulders reminded her of Jamie's square sturdy figure.

He returned her intent regard with a warmly humorous smile. 'I'm pleased to meet you at last, Jan. And I hope I may call you Jan because I have heard so much about you.'

Jan acknowledged his friendly greeting with a strained smile before her eyes turned to Angela, who hurried to his side almost protectively. Jan had thought her beautiful before but now she seemed to glow with an inner radiance and her green eyes had a luminous quality. The red lips which had so often drooped with discontent now curved with a new softness. There was no doubt that the two people before her had found each other again and in doing so their love shone out for all to see.

Jan's heart ached for Mike, standing only a few paces away. She knew the pain of loving someone unattainable. She stole a tentative glance at him and found his gaze fixed broodingly upon herself. He was an inch or two taller than Jim McCall and in his well-cut dark suit he had a commanding air of strength and power. Yet to Jan's observant gaze there were shadows in the depths of his green eyes and an unfamiliar, almost pleading, expression which made him seem unusually vulnerable.

She brought her attention back to Angela with difficulty, as she heard her say, 'What a pity Tim cannot come tonight after all...'

Jan felt her own spirits sink lower then ever. She had been depending on Tim's presence to help her through this last evening of the old year. She saw Mike's eyes narrow as he watched her intently and she turned away to hide the feeling of desolation which threatened to swamp her. The year which was almost over had robbed her of her parents, of the home she had known and loved all her life; soon Chris and Tom would be happily settled in another country, even John seemed happy. What could the new year hold for her? she wondered bleakly. Even during the major crises in her life—Bobby's birth and her parents' deaths—she had never felt so lonely and bereft as she did tonight. The man she loved was at her side and he may as well have been a million miles away.

She moved to greet Jamie, sprawled contentedly on the curly hearthrug. He looked up and her heart jerked at the spontaneous—oh so achingly familiar—crooked grin. Like his mother, Jamie had also aquired a new aura of peace and contentment now that Jim McCall had resumed his rightful place in their lives.

The elaborate meal was served in the long, high-ceilinged diningroom where the oval mahogany table gleamed with the Dunbar silver, and crystal goblets caught and reflected a thousand sparkling colours.

Afterwards Jamie pleaded for a game of "Hunt the Thimble" to which his father agreed with alacrity, then promptly excused himself on account of his head. He gave Jan a conspiratorial wink and claimed her for his companion until the game was over.

He led her across the hall to a smaller sittingroom and settled her comfortably beside the fire before shutting the door firmly. For a few seconds he regarded her quizzically and Jan knew instinctively that he had engineered the opportunity to be alone with her. But why? she wondered uneasily.

'I met your son yesterday,' he remarked casually as he seated himself on the opposite side of the hearth, 'Mike brought him and the twins to see Jamie's new train set.'

'Y-yes. He enjoyed himself.' Jan knew she sounded stilted and tense but Jim McCall's frank, penetrating gaze made her feel strangely apprehensive.

He sighed.

'Yes, as you've probably guessed, Jan, I wanted to speak to you alone. Forgive me if I rush in where angels fear to tread!' He gave a wry grimace. 'As a matter of fact, Angela wanted me to meet Bobby. She thinks he resembles Jamie.' Jan could not stifle her gasp of dismay and she stared at him like a mesmerised rabbit.

'Mm... So you *have* noticed it too...?' he murmured thoughtfully—almost with satisfaction—Jan noticed in amazement.

'Until I saw Bobby for myself I was sure it was all in Angela's mind,' he went on, 'and of course it is just odd wee traits, mannerisms he could have copied, their eyes, a certain way of smiling... It could be coincidence I suppose...?'

'Y-yes,' Jan muttered, staring unseeingly at the brass fire-irons.

'Unless they were related?' Jim McCall suggested softly.

Jan froze. She clenched her fists until her nails bit into her palms. But Jim McCall waited patiently for her response.

'R-related?' she stammered.

'Yes. We, that is Angela and I, wonder if it is a possibility?'

'A-Angela...?' Jan stared at him wide-eyed. 'Then you know!' she whispered and her shoulders slumped. 'You know that Mike is their father?'

Jim McCall smiled gently, compassionately.

'And you...you don't mind!' she breathed incredulously.

Jim McCall held her gaze steadily, then he said quietly, 'You know Mike and I have been close friends for years, but even with the best of friends there are some things a man like Mike would never discuss. That is why I wanted to speak to you alone. But I must apologise for letting you make the admission Angela and I hoped to hear...' Jan stared at him with a puzzled frown. 'As for minding,' he went on, 'I don't have anything to mind about. I *know* that *I* am Jamie's father.'

Jan lowered her eyes but not before he had read the doubts and sympathy in them.

'Obviously you are not convinced...' he sighed. 'I have Angela's permission to tell you anything I consider necessary to clear things up a little. But first I should tell you something of our relationship... I believe Angela has already told you she...er "trapped" me into marriage by becoming pregnant...?'

'Y-yes...she mentioned something like that,' Jan muttered uncomfortably. He grimaced ruefully.

'It's not strictly true. I didn't put up much of a fight. I only resisted at all because I knew Angela was way out of my class—and I suppose I do have more than my fair share of pride and independence. Anyway when we first met, Angela had just returned from a world tour—a whole year of first-class travelling. She looked wonderful! Just like a Grecian goddess—golden suntan, raven hair, beautiful figure—I didn't stand a chance! But she had just blown as much money in one year as I could make in five on a sheep farm—and even then it's a family concern. So I tried avoiding her. But I was staying at Shamlee for the summer and Angela thrives on challenge. It didn't take her long to realise I loved her anyway.' He shrugged helplessly. 'I tried to tell her I had nothing to offer her—not in comparison to her present lifestyle. I vowed I would never accept charity from her parents, or anyone else. We quarrelled over what she called my "stiff-necked pride". But Angela was used to having her own way. She had never been thwarted in her life.' He sighed, 'and I, I must have been weak. I didn't hold out long before I succumbed to the temptations she offered... As I said, Angela knows I'm telling you this, Jan. I'm not being disloyal. I simply found her irresistible... Anyway, the next thing I knew she was pregnant—and I *know* beyond any doubt that I was responsible! At the time I was horrified! So was Mike. He had introduced us you see and Angela made herself out to be far more brazen than she really was—making out it was all a trap. I think she did it in case Mike and I quarrelled.

'I went to see her father. He was very decent...extremely understanding in fact. Angela could be very impulsive, almost wild at times. I think it worried him and he thought I might be a steadying influence. I agreed to marry her but only if she loved me enough to live as my family and I lived—comfortably but without any of the luxuries she had been used to. I didn't hold out much hope that she would agree—and I wondered whether I would be strong enough to stick to my guns. You see Angela had two magnificent horses of her own, for a start. She is an excellent horsewoman and she had been the star of the gymkhanas since she was a toddler. One horse as a hobby was the most I could manage. She had been used to a cook and a housekeeper... I didn't think she could possibly give all that up for me. But she did...'

He smiled and his eyes held a great tenderness. 'We were idyllically happy... Then she came to stay at Glenhead while Mrs Dunbar had her operation. At first I didn't worry when she didn't return. But when I arranged to come down and take her back with me she kept making excuses. I knew the operation had been a phenomenal success... Then I heard that her father had made her a gift of another horse, apparently as an expression of gratitude because she had stayed with her mother and given moral support...'

'Nero!' Jan murmured, remembering the magnificent, mettlesome black stallion with a shudder.

'Yes, Nero!' Jim McCall agreed tight-lipped. 'Mr Dunbar realised Angela was unhappy about something and he resorted to the old habit of trying to buy her happiness. Of course I thought Angela had grown tired of me and my simple style of living. And, God forgive me, I was too proud to come and plead with her to return.' He stared hard at the leaping flames, then, 'Thank goodness Jamie intervened,' he muttered fervently, 'even though he did take such a terrible risk and worry everyone. So,' he looked Jan steadily in the eye, 'you see our problems were not caused by Mike and I *am* Jamie's father. The thing is... I couldn't believe that Mike could possibly be Bobby's father. It is so out of character. He always had more control than any man I knew...and such rigid views too! But the way his eyes follow your every move... I knew there has to be something between you and I know he has been unhappy. I guessed you were the reason he went off to Canada. Now I would like to help him if I can. We owe him everything, and you see...' he took a deep breath. 'I'm beginning to believe Angela and Mike could be related after all—half-brother and sister...to be exact.'

'Brother and sister!' Jan squeaked in astonishment, completely shaken out of her dull lethargy. 'It's not possible— Is it?' she whispered incredulously, staring into the pleasant homely face of Jim McCall, knowing he could not have made up such a story.

He shrugged lightly and a slight frown creased his brow. 'I don't know,' he said slowly, 'Angela is adopted you see...'

'Adopted!' Jan could only echo his words stupidly.

'Yes. We know her natural mother was

Irish. She had lived in this area—one of the reasons the Dunbars came to Glenhead—with her husband and a young son. But she met Mrs Dunbar in a Glasgow hospital. She had been taken there after collapsing at the airport. She was returning from a trip abroad I believe...' He frowned in concentration, marshalling the facts as he must have heard them. 'She had a kidney disease I think. Anyway she knew she was dying and the baby was not her husband's. She pleaded with the Dunbars to look after her. They had just lost their own child. Mrs Dunbar was not so young and knew she could never have another you see. Mr Dunbar made sure everything was done legally by a firm of Glasgow solicitors. Her last request was that the baby should be christened Angela after her father—Angelino. She had money too. Half of it was left in trust for her son to inherit when he reached twenty-one. The rest was for the child's education—the money Angela had "blown" on her world cruise.

'Once the adoption was legal I honestly believe Mrs Dunbar regarded Angela as her own daughter. It was only when she was faced with her operation and knew she might not recover that she told Angela the truth and gave her a gold locket containing a photograph of her real mother and a man. Angela was absolutely shattered apparently. When Mrs Dunbar did recover Angela tried to question her but she pretended it was all a mistake and refused to discuss anything. Angela was afraid to persist in case she caused her to have a relapse. Then she got it into her head that there was something to hide—perhaps her mother had been a criminal or something. She was afraid I would despise her—as if anything could alter my love for her!' Jim McCall groaned. 'But my parents are very religious I suppose—they don't recognise divorce and that sort of thing. She was afraid they would reject her if they knew she was illegitimate... Poor Angie. She can't believe that they love her for herself—and I know that they do.

'In the end she confided in Mike. Thank God she had him! Unfortunately she tied his hands, or rather his tongue, because she swore him to secrecy—and she knew Mike would never break a promise. When she showed him the photograph he thought it resembled his own parents. He wanted to ask Mr Kerr for the family album and a few more details of his own mother but Angela wouldn't agree. She went to Edinburgh to see if she could trace any records but she didn't have much success. Mike tried to persuade her to tell me but she was adamant—and very confused and unhappy I understand.'

'Poor Angela,' Jan murmured feelingly. 'Her whole world must have rocked completely.'

'Aye,' Jim agreed with a heartfelt sigh, 'and the family seems to mean so much to both Angela and Mike. It's almost an obsession with them. There's always been a peculiar empathy between them. I'm afraid I've always taken my family for granted.'

'Yes I know what you mean,' Jan murmured but she was thinking of Mike as a small orphaned boy, probably feeling lonely and rejected by the mother he had loved. Had she intended to return? Was she really Angela's mother too—with the same impulsive determination, the same craving to be loved...?'

Jim McCall broke into her thoughts, 'Well I know I have convinced Angela that it will never change my feelings if she turns out to be the daughter of the devil or the Angel Gabriel himself,' he said with a grin. 'I only hope all this may clear the air between you and Mike in some way—especially if Jamie and Bobby do turn out to share the same grandmother.' Jan smiled. Inside she wanted to jump for joy.

'You have helped me more than you'll ever know,' she said with feeling.

'In that case it's time we returned to the party. After all that talking I need a drink!'

Everyone was watching the Hogmanay party on television when they returned to the lounge but Mike came to her side immediately. Together they watched the dancers weaving in and out of their reels and strathspeys, the tempo increasing the excitement and filling them all with renewed anticipation as the New Year rushed towards them. All Jan's earlier desolation had vanished. In a dream she watched Mr Dunbar handing round the glasses while his wife plied everyone with shortbread and black bun. Jan felt Mike's eyes on her and looked up into his face. The intense yearning which blazed like a green fire set her trembling in response. Big Ben began to chime. The room was filled with laughter and cheers. Everyone was clinking glasses and exchanging toasts.

Mike lowered his dark head but his eyes held a silent query. Jan smiled radiantly, all her inhibitions had disappeared as she lifted her face eagerly to meet his kiss—so brief but so poignantly sweet. Was it a silent promise for the year ahead?

'Will you walk back to Shamlee with me, Jan? Over the fields?' he whispered urgently. She nodded as Tom and Jim and even Mr Dunbar came to claim their kisses and exchange good wishes.

When they were linking hands to sing *Auld Lang Syne* she placed her own in Mike's hand and felt his fingers tighten—strong and warm and reassuring. The fire in his hooded eyes sent the blood pulsing through her veins like a rushing tide. She listened as his deep rich voice rang out exultantly:

And here's a hand my trusty freen'
And gie's hand o' thine,

Was it possible that he could want her hand in his—always?

Amidst the general hubbub of laughter and good wishes Mike drew her from the room, urging her into her coat and furlined boots.

214

Together they stepped out into the crystal silence of another world and another year. Their feet crunched on the silver carpet of frosted grass gleaming in the light of the full moon. Jan drew in great breaths of the clear exhilarating air.

'The moon is like a silver galleon sailing on a star-studded sea,' she murmured, her voice husky with the wonder and beauty of the world around them yet still half-afraid that this evening might be just a dream, a fairy tale which would end and snatch away her fragile hopes.

'Whenever and wherever I have seen that moon, Jan, I have always thought of you. In Canada it seemed to hang like a magnificent silver medallion just above the treetops—but always out of reach, just like the slender laughing girl in a primrose gown who continually haunted my memory.' Jan was quiet, awed by the depth of sincerity in his voice. 'I have a confession to make,' he said and his fingers tightened as she stiffened involuntarily. 'I asked Tim to stay away tonight.'

'Tim? But why?'

Mike hesitated. When he spoke his words came out slowly.

'I had to talk to you—alone. I thought

this might be my last chance. I had written to Tom and Chris, asking them to return and settle the question of Shamlee. After the night of the dance I knew I could never keep my promise to Tom or maintain the status quo. I had to be free to talk to you—to have something definite to offer you—and Bobby.

'But then I heard you speaking on the telephone...to Johnathan White...' He shuddered. 'I thought you were arranging your *own* wedding—to him. Then you told Chris he was marrying your friend and I knew I had jumped to the wrong conclusion...' he groaned with disgust, 'again! But there was still Tim and all he has to offer you and Bobby. This time I knew there was no room for mistakes—or my stupid pride. I went to see him and asked him to stay away—for this one evening. I told him you had always been the only girl in my life...' Jan gasped incredulously. 'I have no pride left where you are concerned Jan!' he insisted on a note of desperation. 'I need you! Anyway after some persuasion Tim reluctantly agreed to give me this one chance. He muttered something about Bobby always looking vaguely familiar, even the first time he saw him on the train—and now he knew the reason...'

He stopped and turned her to face him and even through her thick sheepskin coat Jan felt the steely grip of his fingers, hard with tension. 'Jan...?'

She nodded. 'Yes Bobby is your son, Mike. There has never been anyone else. Jim McCall guessed too...'

'Jim? He *asked* you...?' Mike prompted indignantly.

'Oh I don't mind—not now... You see he told me so much more in exchange—about Angela...that you regard her as a sister. Oh Mike... I've been so jealous of her! So mixed up too...I thought you were Jamie's father as well as Bobby's...'

'Ach Jan! My own darling Jan...' He pulled her close and wrapped his arms around her tenderly as though he would protect her from every ill the world had to offer. 'There could never be anyone but you...' he groaned softly, burying his face in her silky hair then in the warm hollow of her neck. For a while they stood together—holding each other close—quite unable to believe in their new-found freedom to speak honestly and openly of their mutual love—savouring the miracle

217

of rediscovering their first early rapture and the promise of so much more.

At last Mike put a finger beneath the small determined chin which he had grown to love. He tilted her face to receive his kiss and with it all the love and tenderness he had withheld so long. When he eventually lifted his head he pressed her trembling body even closer.

'Can you ever forgive me Jan, for all my doubts—all the unhappiness I have caused you?'

Jan raised her hand to trace the strong contours of his face as she had so often longed to do. Her fingers smoothed away the lines and moved wonderingly over the firm lips whose kisses thrilled her very soul.

'I love you so much. I have been so lonely and miserable at the thought of leaving you,' she murmured huskily.

'Then you will marry me Jan?' She felt the surge of relief and exultant joy which seemed to vibrate through his powerful body and into her own.

'You...will not feel trapped?' she asked gently.

'Trapped! Dear Jan there never was a more willing victim. Never a man more eager to enter the tender trap of matrimony with you.' He cradled her cool face in his hands and kissed her, over and over again as though he would make up for the years of longing. The fires of passion mingled and flared instantly, melting every lingering particle of uncertainty until Jan clung to him helplessly.

They walked in a dream over the sparkling fields, talking, stopping, laughing, kissing. Young lovers in a world filled only with the moon and stars, with a new year and a new life ahead of them.

As they reached the last gate, Mike stopped and pulled her once more into his arms.

'I'm almost afraid you'll fly away with the magic of the night,' he whispered huskily, 'just as you flew away from me that sunny Sunday morning five years ago. As soon as you turned from me I knew I had made the biggest mistake of my life in judging you as other women. I knew then that you were very, very special—and so innocent it was unbelievable. Tell me, Jan...when I wrote to you begging you to marry me—why did you never answer my letters? Even to put me out of my misery?'

219

Jan was silent. Stunned.

'You...you asked me to marry you—then, Mike?'

'But of course! Oh I knew you said you didn't want to see me again—and I deserved that after the cruel, cynical accusations I had made. I told you all I knew about my family, all that was in my heart. Searching for any excuse if you could only forgive me... Half of me knew I had no right. I knew you were in the middle of your college course—and enjoying it. But I was dismayed when I realised you were barely eighteen! To me you seemed all woman—my woman, and I had taken advantage of your girl's innocence. But I couldn't forget you! Why didn't you reply Jan? Even to my second letter—just asking to see you again, promising I would wait until you were through college if that was your wish?'

'I...I didn't open the first letter. It came so soon afterwards...I felt so confused. Our time together...everything had seemed so wonderful! But I felt I had been cheap, that I...' She heard Mike's indrawn breath of protest but she went on. 'I thought I could put you out of my mind... Banish the memory... Later, when the second letter came I had begun to realise there was something wrong...I couldn't take it in. I couldn't believe I was pregnant. It was a long time before I could tell my parents... After the first shock—they were wonderful. But Mike, don't you see? If they had guessed they would have let you know—somehow, through Chris. You would have felt pressurised into marrying me—like your father perhaps...? and Jim McCall? I couldn't bear the thought of forcing you into a marriage without love...'

He groaned and buried his face in her hair, 'It would not have been without love—not for me!' He hugged her tightly as though suddenly afraid she might change her mind—even now.

Jan reached up and pulled his face close to her own. 'I love you with all my heart Mike,' she murmured against his lips. 'I think I always have and I know I always will. Bobby will be proud you are his father. We are yours Mike—your own kith and kin from now on, my darling.' She pressed her lips to his, sealing her words with a tender kiss.

Mike's arms tightened as he took command, drawing a response which left them both weak with desire. At last he held her gently from him.

'Come my little one, I want to tell everyone our news. I think Papa Kerr will be almost as happy as we are ourselves. As for Chris and Tom, it's a good job they are staying at Shamlee just now I'm thinking! Janet Anne Carron...' he murmured her full name wonderingly. 'I cannae believe you'll soon be mine—wholly mine—at last!'

Rosy colour suffused Jan's cheeks at the vibrant urgency in his husky voice. She looked up into the strong planes of his beloved face, etched clearly against the moonlight, and caught the gleam of raw desire in his compelling eyes—eyes which held so many secret promises for the woman he loved—herself.

'You will marry me *soon*, Jan?'

'Very soon!' she echoed fervently.

The publishers hope that this book has given you enjoyable reading. Large Print Books are especially designed to be as easy to see and hold as possible. If you wish a complete list of our books, please ask at your local library or write directly to: Dales Large Print Books, Long Preston, North Yorkshire, BD23 4ND, England.

This Large Print Book for the Partially sighted, who cannot read normal print, is published under the auspices of

THE ULVERSCROFT FOUNDATION